Deep OverstOck

#12: Mysteries
April 2021

> "The possession of knowledge does not kill the sense of wonder and mystery. There is always more mystery."
>
> *Anaïs Nin*

MYST - MYSTERY

Editorial

Editors-In-Chief: Mickey Collins & Robert Eversmann

Managing Editor: Z.B. Wagman

Poetry: Jihye Shin

Prose: Z.B. Wagman

Cover: Hannah Collins

Contact: editors@deepoverstock.com
deepoverstock.com

On the Shelves

7 Nothing Bad Without Good - Joe Giordano

18 Lycophron of Chalcis - Jonathan van Belle

20 Foxwoman: An Ancient Folk Mystery - Yuan Changming

21 Woman in Elevator, Paris - Roger Camp

22 Salient Green - Nancy Hayes

29 A Model Murder - Z.B. Wagman

31 The Barrel - Holly Day

36 Ode to the Manifesto Written on a Chrysler Pacifica in a Barnes and Noble Parking Lot - Lindsay Granduke

38 Exchanged - Lynette G. Esposito

40 The Art of Detection - Kate Falvey

45 Love Languages - Nicole Chvatal

46 for - Mark D Cart

47 The Mole People - Mickey Collins

50 Bodie - Sherry Shahan

51 FLY BOTTLE - Jonathan van Belle

55 Flocci Volitantes: A Metaphysical Mystery - Yuan Changming

56 History of Knotted Artifacts - Mike Corrao

64 The Ghost in the Attic Closet - Charles Halsted

65 The King's Man - Ben Crowley

77 Death Comes to the old Lady, Paris - Roger Camp

78 Heartfelt Confusion: A Personal Puzzle - Yuan Changming

79 Von Zimmer 2805 - Nicole Chvatal

80 The Case of the Radiator - Bob Selcrosse

91 sure - Mark D Cart

92 Not Waving if You Look Long Enough - Alex Werner

102 Murder at Murphy Manor - Timothy Arliss OBrien

104 Who Killed the Middle Class? - L. Fid

116 Whistling in the Dark - Nicholas Yandell

118 The Art of the Never-Ending Ego - Kate Falvey

119 One Thing I Won't Forget - Karla Linn Merrifield

continued...

continued...

120 A Glimmer of Intuition - Jen Mierisch

132 Mystery Outpost VII - Vincent A. Alascia

137 The Disappearance - Mickey Collins

139 The Case of the Disposal - Bob Selcrosse

Letter from the Editors

Dearest readers,

This issue is chock-full of clues for you to follow and mysteries to solve. We've got mysteries in barrels and mysteries aboard outposts in outer space, mysteries in artifacts, mysteries in notebooks and mysteries in fox women and cat women too. We've got detectives in the style of Poe and Chandler, and even detectives who are children. Whodunit? Youdunit!

But the biggest mystery of all is how the heck did we decide on which ones to keep from all of the great submissions? As Sherlock Holmes would deduce, the simplest solution is probably the correct one; and the simplest answer is that we ran out of pages!

Our next theme is the future! Submit before the deadline is in the past, that is to say, by May 31st.

See you some time in the land of tomorrow!

Deep Overstock Editors

Nothing Bad Without Good
by Joe Giordano

Killers had become brazen. Wednesday afternoon around 2 p.m., a gunman firing from the passenger side of a car shot a man on the sidewalk walking beside a ten-year-old girl. As Thomas Green collapsed, bleeding out on the pavement, the murderer grabbed his sister Chyna, jumped back into the car and the driver took off. I arrived at the crime scene as the medical team examined Green's body, a few steps from Sal's—the Bensonhurst home of the best Italian pastries in Brooklyn. The lens on the block's security camera had been spray-painted, but another pair of eyes were present. Sal had long given up the day-to-day running of the business to his son and daughter-in-law, but each day he sat at a small table outside the picture window, greeting customers, and kibitzing with passing neighbors.

The female cop reported that witnesses, including Sal, couldn't describe the killer or report the car's license plate. My gaze turned to him, nursing a tumbler of red wine, and decided we needed to talk. I'm Bragg, a gold-shield detective out of Brooklyn South.

Well into his nineties, thin, with a full head of white hair, Sal evaluated me with clear brown eyes. I flashed my badge and asked if I could sit. At the sight of my shield, his face soured. Not a cop lover.

He asked in a raspy voice, "You Italian?"

I wanted Sal's cooperation, and I hoped to break through his crusty attitude by answering honestly. "Can't say. I didn't know my father, and my mother never spoke of him."

"If he gave you those blue eyes, he could've been from Palermo." He motioned for me to sit. "So, Detective Paisan," he nicknamed me, "I already told the patrolwoman I didn't see anything."

I tried another tack. After all, most people love to complain. "I'm guessing you had a bad experience with cops," I said. "Care to tell me about it?"

He huffed, then paused to sip his wine, probably deciding what he'd reveal.

"When I was eighteen, my uncle Nunzio sponsored my emigration to the States," he began. "He owned a small fishing boat in San Francisco. A kind man, he'd been coaching me on my duties at sea for just a few months when he suffered a heart attack and died."

"My sympathies," I said.

Sal nodded. "He left me his boat, an incredible gesture. Suddenly, I found myself with the means to earn an independent living, and my emotions were bittersweet. My uncle had treated me like a son, and I mourned his death, but I also felt elated over his bequest."

"Nothing bad without good," I said.

"Very philosophical," he responded in a wry tone. "Unfortunately, the year was 1942. WWII was raging and Italians became classified as enemy aliens. San Francisco was a strategic port, and Italian fishermen had to leave. A couple of Federal agents confiscated the boat, and I was taken into custody and deported to an internment camp in Texas."

"A sad period in our history."

"Ever been to Texas?" he asked rhetorically. "Hot as Mount Etna without a view of the Mediterranean." He scoffed. "And the food." He scrunched up his face before taking a gulp of wine, presumably to blot away the memory.

"How did you get to New York?" I asked.

"Upon my release, I learned the boat had been wrecked. A cousin in New York recommended me to a boss, and I became a numbers runner for a Little Italy mob until," he raised his hands expansively, "I earned the money to open this place."

"You bounced back. Good for you."

He nodded.

I hoped my attentiveness had oiled his cooperation and asked, "Do you want to tell me what you saw today?"

"What, you're done buttering me up already?" he asked with mock surprise.

I sat back, pausing a moment, then decided to be blunt. "The shooter saw you. Do you think he'll trust you to stay silent? More likely, he'll want you dead."

He shrugged in a way that told me he'd already come to the same conclusion. "How much would he shorten my life?" He lifted his glass. "At my age, if the wine shop tells me a red is better to drink next year, I don't buy it."

I played my last card, hoping to tug at Sal's humanity. "A child has been kidnapped."

He puffed out a long breath, then spoke in a resigned tone. "I'm not under any illusions about these people. You're right, they might kill me for insurance. And I'd like to help the little girl. But if I talk," he leaned closer and his thumb jerked toward his son and daughter-in-law serving customers in the shop, "the bastard will kill them too."

***

While two cops made the death notice to Thomas Green's family, I consulted with my boss, Lieutenant Dixon, a grizzled African American.

"I've already contacted the FBI to recover the child," he said, "Agent Maxwell will meet you at the Green family home, but you focus on the murder."

"The age of the victim suggests the killing could've been gang related, perhaps a dispute over a drug territory."

"A plausible hypothesis," Dixon said, then leaned back

sticking his thumbs under his belt, "but snatching the kid is odd. Ransom might've been the main motive."

"Unless Thomas Green stashed away a pile of drug money, the family won't have much cash for the kidnappers."

"And we'll find the girl dead in an alley," Dixon said glumly. "Get on it and keep me updated."

***

I arranged to meet FBI Special Agent Maxwell at the Green home. Beardless with a crew cut, he wore a cheap Men's Wearhouse suit, which still fit better than mine. Walking up the drive, we passed a red Porsche 911 and a blue BMW convertible that were probably worth more than the asphalt shingle home we approached.

Thomas's mother, early forties, appeared jittery and was frowning with worry when she opened the door and saw our credentials. We expressed our sympathy for the loss of her son.

She wiped her eyes saying, "I just received a call from Chyna's kidnappers." Her voice rose. "They want $250,000 for her release and no FBI involvement."

Maxwell and I exchanged glances before I said to her, "May we talk inside."

She hesitated, then led us into her kitchen and offered us coffee, which we declined. Her seventeen-year-old son, Lionel, sporting a dour expression, slouched in the chair next to her.

The phone tap we ordered hadn't been established, so Maxwell asked, "What exactly did the kidnappers say?"

Mrs. Green took a moment, then spoke slowly. "If you want to see your daughter alive, give us $250,000. Don't involve the FBI or we'll kill her." Her eyes widened with alarm. "Could they know you're here?"

Two white guys in suits showing up at her door would certainly have been clocked as cops by anyone watching the house, but I sought to reassure her. "Working with the FBI is your best chance to get Chyna back."

"With your permission," Maxwell said, "I'd like to have some technicians set up another phone so I can listen in when the kidnappers call back. They'll give you instructions for dropping off the money, and I'll coach you how to respond."

Mrs. Green cupped her forehead. "But I don't have $250,000."

"Let's take things one step at a time," Maxwell responded. "May I bring in my people?"

Mrs. Green glanced quickly at her son before nodding agreement.

While Maxwell stepped away to call his office, I took the opportunity to ask, "Do you know anyone who would've wanted to hurt Thomas?"

Lionel broke eye contact.

Mrs. Green shook her head saying, "He wouldn't speak to me about what he did on the streets, but he always had money, and I worried how he came by it."

"Were drugs ever brought into the house?"

"Never," Mrs. Green said sternly.

Lionel didn't look as certain, so I pressed further. "Might Thomas have been dealing drugs?"

Mrs. Green puffed out a breath, then placed a hand on her son's shoulder. "I admit, that was my fear."

I turned to Lionel, "Do you know if Thomas was dealing drugs?"

He shook his head, but I wasn't convinced. I fought off the instinct to lecture him not to follow his brother's path. He might've already been hip deep in the business. Fast cars, women, nightlife, respect from homies were the temptations of drug trafficking for too many kids, living for the present and never reflecting that the infamous often died young.

While Maxwell continued to confer with his technical support, Mrs. Green walked me to the door. She took my hand in both of hers. "Please. Bring my baby back home."

My overwhelming urge was to try to relieve the woman's anguish by guaranteeing success. Instead, I told her the truth. "I'll do my best."

Lieutenant Dixon had told me to focus on the homicide, but the killer was also the kidnapper, and I wasn't stepping aside for the FBI.

***

Back in my car, I pondered my next step. Sal was my best hope to get the killer's description, but he was understandably concerned for his family. Offering them witness protection would mean they'd need to abandon the bakery which Sal wouldn't buy. Without his cooperation, I couldn't get authorization to station cops at his home or the shop. All I could do was ask the local police patrol to keep an eye on him.

I had one other possibility to get Sal some protection, and perhaps a lead on Thomas Green's killer. A long shot and a distasteful option to pursue, but if the gambit could lead to Chyna's recovery, I had to bite down and try it.

Italian and American flags flapped over the doorway of the brick Italian American Club in Bensonhurst. I flashed my badge at the door and stepped inside. The muted-light interior smelled of cigars, and the walls had a few large photos of famous Italian Americans including Rocky Marciano and Joe DiMaggio. Sitting at a corner table like a Roman emperor, Cosimo Ruggiero, the eponymous boss of the Ruggiero Crime Family, held court. He was five eight and slim, with thick hands gnarled by once-broken middle knuckles. His mane of silver accentuated his Florida tan.

As I approached, he recognized me and waved away the

others at his table.

He didn't rise. "Detective Bragg, unexpected, but I can't say a pleasure. You here for a donation to the policeman's ball or some shit?"

I took a seat without being asked. "What can you tell me about the shooting outside Sal's?"

Ruggiero looked amused. "Just like that? No pleasant chitchat?"

"The murderer grabbed a child." I couldn't summon up a friendly tone with this prick. "Time is wasting."

He raised his mangled hands. "I'm to become a police informant to save a little girl. How noble."

"What do you know about what went down?"

His tone feigned innocence. "Only what I read in the *New York Post*."

"Cut the bullshit."

He stiffened, and his tone became sharp. "You have some nerve waltzing in here expecting me to be your stoolie."

"You're not upset that the killing happened in your neighborhood?"

"If I was," he waved disrespectfully, "I'd handle it without your encouragement."

"Sal Amico witnessed the shooting."

"So I hear." He leaned forward. "His *sfogliatelle*, hot from the oven," he smacked his lips before sitting back, "try them. You'll thank me."

I held my temper. "Sal won't tell me what he witnessed. The killer won't care and gun for him."

Ruggiero cocked his head. "Did Sal tell you he was a numbers runner in the old days?" He scoffed. "That guy was a force before he hung up his spikes."

I'd come for a reason. "Will you put out the word that he's under your protection?"

"You know," he spoke philosophically, "in the wars we wage, there are no winners and losers."

My eyebrows rose.

He continued. "The winners kill all the losers." He chuckled at his macabre joke. "I don't start a war unless I know I'll win. Declaring myself for Sal chooses a side, and I'm not getting in the middle of a conflict."

"You'll leave Sal hanging."

He shrugged. "I hope he taught his son and daughter-in-law all he knows about pastry. You know. Just in case."

Heat rose up my neck. I wanted to threaten the arrogant prick, but bluster was the refuge for the weak. Without another word, I stood and strode from the club.

Back in the car, still steaming from my confrontation with Ruggiero, I received a call from Lieutenant Dixon.

"Meet Maxwell at the McDonald's on Bay Parkway. The kidnappers have made contact."

***

As I approached him in a parking lot filled with police cars and flashing light bars, Maxwell's face was grim.

"A customer found this in the men's room." He held a coffee cup with the name "Chyna" scrawled on the outside. Inside, was a piece of a child's ear.

"Jesus Christ," I blurted at the grisly display.

He handed the cup to forensics and walked me over to his computer. "This thumb drive was included. No prints." The drive was plugged into his laptop. "Listen to this," he said.

The voice was purposely distorted. "At 3 a.m. on Thursday, leave $250,000 in a satchel at Bensonhurst park on the corner of Cropsey and Bay Ridge Parkway. Only five and ten dollar bills. Old notes. No GPS trackers. No dye packs. Don't follow unless you want to find the kid in a trash bag."

The recording continued with what Mrs. Green later confirmed was Chyna's voice. "They cut me. Please pay the money. Mommy, I love you."

"Son of a bitch," I said.

"They must've seen us at the house," Maxwell said, "and decided not to communicate by phone."

"They're not negotiating," I said, "just giving orders and this sounds like the last message we'll receive."

Maxwell huffed agreement.

I turned for my car and he called out. "Where are you going?"

Pausing at the door, I said, "I need to make another run at the eyewitness to the kidnapping." I jumped into my car and took off for Sal's.

***

Halfway to the bakery, Dixon called. "Sal Amico's been shot. They took him to New York Community Hospital. Get over there."

Inside the Emergency Room's waiting area, Sal's son and daughter-in-law held each other. She was in tears, his face in obvious distress. I approached them and he choked out, "He's gone."

"I'm so sorry." Frustration and a feeling of helplessness boiled my gut.

A patrolwoman pulled me aside. "We found him lying in a

pool of blood where he normally sat, in front of the bakery."

"He probably saw his attacker approach."

She nodded. "His vintage belly gun, a .38 revolver, was under the body. He got off two shots. I found blood droplets leading to the street, likely from his assailant."

A doctor in blue scrubs emerged and said something to the family. Afterward, he spotted us and approached.

"Mr. Amico had this in his pocket."

His gloved hand held a bloodstained, sealed envelope with the words written on the outside, "For Detective Paisan."

I put on gloves and retrieved the contents. He'd written on a slip of paper a license plate number and the name, "Big Ed Cowan," a known drug kingpin, followed by, "Nothing bad without good."

I swallowed the emotion in my throat and phoned Lieutenant Dixon.

"Sal identified the murderer," I said. "Should be as good as a deathbed confession for a judge." The plate led to a stolen car, a dead end, but we knew the house where Cowan and his crew hung out.

"I'll get the warrant and summon up a SWAT team," Dixon said. "We'll be ready in an hour. Meet us at the gang headquarters. I'll call Maxwell."

I was right behind the SWAT team when they broke through the door. No shots were fired as they spread through the house. The thugs were cuffed without much struggle. We found the hitman, dead, lying on bloodied sheets with two slugs inside him we later confirmed were from Sal's pistol. Cowan tried to escape out a window. I grabbed him and threw him to the floor. A member of SWAT helped, and I cuffed him.

"Where's Chyna," I shouted in his face.

"Who?"

"The little girl, you son of a bitch."

He smirked. "I want a lawyer."

I turned him over to another cop and was about to do a room-to-room search of my own, when one of the SWAT members shouted, "She's here," and I rushed over.

Chyna lay inside a closet with a crude bloodstained bandage wrapped around her head. She had the most frightened eyes I'd ever seen. Her mouth, hands, and feet were duct taped. I scooped her into my arms, and she cried as I gently freed her.

"Mommy's waiting," I said as I carried her to the ambulance outside. As I handed her over to the EMT, I hoped he didn't see that my tears had welled.

***

Sal's wake was standing room only. At the bier, he looked smaller inside a frilly bed of white and oak. When I expressed my sympathies to his son and commented on the crowd, he teared up, telling me, "He had a lot of friends."

I nodded. Me among them.

Ruggiero showed up with a contingent of his goons. People parted like the Red Sea as he made his way forward. He'd sent the largest flower arrangement. Bastard. I turned in the opposite direction.

For the next few months, whenever I'd frequent Sal's, I'd glance at his table, mumbling a *buon giorno* and imagining his response. But the pastries and *macchiato* never tasted quite as good, and I found myself going less and less, and finally not at all.

Lycophron of Chalcis
by Jonathan van Belle

Lycophron of Chalcis was appointed by Ptolemy II Philadelphus, son of Ptolemy I Soter, to manage the comedies of the Library of Alexandria, which likely precipitated his scholarly treatise *On Comedy*. Yet Lycophron's own dramatic compositions, with the exception of one satyric drama, *Menedemus*, were tragedies, not comedies.

Lycophron is my favorite mystery. A tragedian tasked with cataloguing comedies; that itself is *tragicomic*. When did Lycophron ink his first tragedies?—before or after Ptolemy's commission? If before, was the commission Ptolemy's joke? If after, was too much laughter poisonous for Lycophron?

There is a third option. Might we suppose tragedy was comedy to this librarian of Alexandria's labyrinth.

"Here," wrote the American philosopher William James, "is the core of the religious problem: *Help*! *Help*!"

"Comedy," said Jerry Lewis, "is a man in trouble."

Pair those and ask: can the core of the religious problem—*our* ultimate problem—be comic? For James, the answer is no: "The divine shall mean for us only such a primal reality as the individual feels impelled to respond to solemnly and gravely, and neither by a curse nor a jest."

Yet, can that core be tragicomic? Jestfully grave?

Lycophron, whom I imagine as a Friedrich Dürrenmatt for the third century B.C.E., perhaps inked a second treatise, a sequel to his *On Comedy*, perhaps titled *On Divine Comedy*, a treatise (dedicated to Momus) now lost, in which his broodings on the *tragic* core of the religious problem effervesce into a laugh at our utter helplessness—into a *tragicomic* affirmation of life.

And later, perhaps Lycophron, without any change in his official commission, began to catalogue tragedies, his own and others, under the heading of comedies. Perhaps Lycophron reasoned as follows: whosoever might catch my miscataloging, would understand my joke, would be a fellow Momus (daresay I, even a devoted "Momist"), and we could double over in black laughter. But who will discover me? I do it so infrequently, and for obscure works, the unsought works. And who, even getting this far, would think it an *intentional* misplacement? And *my* misplacement, at that. Well, that is how it must go. As Empedocles leapt into the molten of Mount Etna, as proof of his deathlessness, so I into the disordering of this library.

Come soon, my reader, my Momus.

Foxwoman: An Ancient Folk Mystery
by Yuan Changming

There is a fairytale told, and retold again
In the Ming Dynasty, about a coquettish fox that
Takes on the shape of a beautiful young woman
Ready to offer herself to a poor obscure guy

Like a magician she brings rich food and wine
To him during the day, and uses her two mouths
To suck up all his yuanqi (energy or masculinity)
At night until he dies in ecstasy of sexual love

Then, the immortal woman would marry another
While many hungry boys would rather become
That lucky guy. I enjoy thinking of that fox
Like a deformed soul wearing a human mask

With hair behind, which makes it feel itchy
While all men are waiting, in anxiety

Woman in Elevator, Paris - Roger Camp

Salient Green
by Nancy Hayes

The ring-a-ding-ding of the bell dangling from the deli shop's front door knob signaled the arrival of yet another customer. Felicity called out a welcome from behind the cash register as the calico made her way to the counter.

"Ooooh, corned beef!" squealed the calico. "What a lovely surprise. I'll take a half a pound, please. Oh, and how about half a pound of the roast beef, a quarter pound of the salami and a whole meatloaf."

From behind the deli case, Claude licked his paws clean, wiped them dry on his crimson-splotched apron then weighed and wrapped the calico's selections. "Here you go, miss. Enjoy!" The calico eagerly accepted the four packages and sauntered over to the register. Felicity rang up her order and smiled as she watched the calico skip out of the shop.

Moments later, the front door jingle-jangled again as an orange tabby made his way in. Felicity beamed at her father. "My goodness! Business is booming. I don't know how you managed to fill the deli case shelves, what with meat being so hard to come by these days, but ever since you did, it's one customer after another."

Claude gazed upon his beautiful daughter, his green eyes twinkling with pride and adoration. "I can't take all the credit, my love. The shelves wouldn't be full if it weren't for the team."

"Speaking of which, um, where's Chuck? I thought he was going to work today."

Claude flashed an uneasy smile. "Didn't I tell you, honey? He's moved on—to, uh, a better place. But, don't worry. We'll be filling his spot in the deli soon."

Claude noticed the orange tabby lingering near the front door. "Welcome to DeliCat, Essen. What can I get for you, today, sir?"

The orange tabby glanced around the shop, taking in the deli's lunch tables, which were filled with boisterous, buoyant customers, before approaching the counter. "Actually, I'm hoping I can do something for you. I noticed your 'Help Wanted' ad in the window. I'm new in town and looking for work. Name's Lance."

Claude gave the tabby a once-over and nodded. "I must say, you look like a big, beefy fellow, Lance. Someone who'd do well at the meat counter. Yes. Let's give you a try."

****

A few days later, on what was now a normal, bustling day at the deli, a group of regulars entered the shop and settled into their usual table. Felicity and Lance, completely absorbed by one another's company, continued to whisper and giggle at the register. After trying and failing to get Felicity's attention, Claude huffed in annoyance, grabbed a notepad and pen, and strode over to the table to wait on the customers.

"Hey, guys. Good to see you as always. So, what will you all be having today?" Claude prompted.

A Maine Coon looked over at his lunch companions, who, in turn, nodded their heads in unison, prodding Tristan to speak for them. "Ahem. Before we launch into our lunch order, we want to thank you for giving us a place to not only meet, but also m.e.a.t. After last year's great cow die-off, we gave up hope we'd ever sink our teeth into a sumptuous, juicy burger again."

Claude accepted their kind words with a bit of discomfiture. "Yeah, admittedly, things became tougher than a vending machine chicken-fried steak after the humans heated up the earth to such a degree the world's poor, burpy cows spontaneously combusted."

Tristan shuddered, "Abominable."

"A bomb in a heifer, too," pointed out Claude. "But thanks to the contributions of my employees, I've been able to keep the

Salient Green   23

deli case fully stocked."

The quartet of felines nodded. "And yet," interjected Timothy, a handsome tuxedo cat, "I'm somewhat surprised you speak so highly of them. They don't seem to stick around for long."

Claude shrugged. "Working at the deli--with me--is not the slice of life everyone seeks. My employees need to be able to take a ribbing."

"Well, here's hoping your new guy stays on," Timothy cheered. "After all, your daughter's quite taken with him, I see."

Claude frowned. "Maybe so, but he likely will be gone soon enough. The daily grind gets to them all eventually."

****

The hair inside Felicity's ears twitched. *Grind? Ribbing? Slice?* "Oh my gosh," she muttered to herself. "The reason the deli's down to a skeleton crew is because Daddy's been giving our fellow workers the ax!"

Felicity raced to the backroom where she found Lance examining a piece of new equipment. "Lance! What are you doing?"

"Hunh? Oh, hi Felicity. I was just checking out the new meat slicer. Your dad promised to put me through a trial run tonight."

Felicity shook her head. "No! Tell him no."

"What? Why would I tell him no, Felicity?"

"Don't you see? Don't you get it? Daddy has plans for you."

"Isn't it great? I've been working here less than a week and he already wants to show me the guts of the operation."

"Exactly!" shrieked Felicity.

Lance grimaced. "Felicity, you're not making sense. This is

good news, a great opportunity. Your dad wants me to be part of the deli."

"Yes, I know. And that's why you've got to leave and go far far away. Daddy's been running through our employees—"

"Which is a lucky break for me."

Felicity sputtered, "Please, let me finish. He's not just running through employees, he's been running employees through the meat grinder!"

"Felicity! That's crazy talk."

"Then where are they, Lance? They disappeared, and all of a sudden meat appears in the deli case."

"Oh, Felicity. You're so cute when you're hysterical. Your father's not a killer. Sure, he has sharp claws, sharp teeth, and spends his days with sharp knives, but he's a pussycat."

Claude poked his head into the backroom. "Oh, there you are, Lance. Are we still on to talk about the special project tonight?"

Lance called out, "Yes, sir! I'll be here."

"Great. Until then, we've got lunch to serve. Chop chop."

Felicity sighed in exasperation. She would just have to take matters into her own two paws.

****

Felicity stormed out of the shop and trod upon the streets until she came to the spot marked on a map given to her long ago by a friend of a friend of a friend who knew a guy who was friends with an underground group of do-gooder rebels. She knelt down onto the asphalt, hoisted a manhole cover up and set it aside. Peering into the hole, she saw nothing but the faint shadow of a ladder. She gulped, pirouetted and started making her way down down down, into the darkness, until her feet sensed the presence of a platform. She positioned herself onto four paws and crawled her way through the city sewer system, looking and listening for signs of the Fortress of the Froglodistes, the legendary group of mutinous vegetarians she'd heard about but whom she'd never wholly believed truly existed.

As Felicity continued to paw her way through the black void, a raspy voice broke the silence.

"Halt. Who goes there?" A torch suddenly burst into fiery life, revealing two bugged-out eyes and a gigantic mouth.

Felicity stammered, "My my name's Felicity. I've come to enlist the help of the Froglodistes."

"Speaking…"

"Oh, ga ga good. Can you take me to your leader?"

The two buggy eyes blinked slowly, while the giant mouth announced, "He's in the process of croaking."

"Oh," mewled Felicity. "I'm sorry to hear that."

"Enh, he's probably done by now. I'll go get him."

The light left with the eyes and mouth, leaving Felicity to wait and tremble in the murky emptiness.

"Crowohhhhoak. You called?" bellowed the Big Froghuna.

Felicity turned in the direction of the guttural voice. "Greetings. I come from the land above ground, where the great cow die-off led to a catastrophic meat shortage, which, in turn, led to desperate beings performing desperate, unspeakable acts."

"Yes, I know of these grim events and dire times. I and my band of fellow Froglodistes fled your world to create a harmonious sanctuary underground."

Felicity pointlessly nodded in the dark. "Yes, that's why I'm here. Your peace-loving ways are well known. I'm hoping your commitment to kindness will spur you to help me."

The Big Froghuna grunted. "And what is this mission you would have us undertake, missy?"

"It's my father. I love him, and I don't want any harm to come to him, but I also love Lance. I fear my father intends to kill him tonight for meat! As vegetarian rebels, I'm hopeful you'll take up my cause and help me save Lance!"

The Big Froghuna chortled. "Where'd you hear that bit of baloney? Vegetarian? Pfft. Why would we be vegetarians when we can eat sweet, juicy insects? They're a nutritious sustainable diet that's all the buzz these days." The Big Froghuna flicked out his long, pink, sticky tongue and lassoed a blue bottle fly. "Nevertheless, we're happy to be part of your swat team. Count us in."

****

Meanwhile, back at the deli, Claude locked the front door and turned the window sign from "Open" to "Closed."

"Thank you for staying late, Lance. I've been impressed with what you've put into the business and would like to see if you're cut out for a new position."

"I'd like that, sir."

"Great. Let's go into the backroom and bone up on the new slicer."

****

Felicity and the Froglodistes arrived at the deli to the grating sound of metallic whirring and the heavenly aroma of barbecue sauce.

"Follow me, guys. I've got a key to the back door." Felicity and her green dream team sped around the building and, at Felicity's "Now!" stormed into the backroom, where they found Claude clutching a knife dripping with dark red ooze.

Upon seeing the posse, Claude gasped. "Felicity! You shouldn't be here…"

"Father! What's going on? Where's Lance?"

Claude pleaded, "Please, go. I don't want you to see this."

"Oh father, what have you done?" sobbed Felicity.

Claude crumpled to the floor. "I wanted to protect you; I'd hoped you'd never find out, although it was for you. I did it all for you."

"How can you say that? I loved Lance. And he loved me. We were going to marry…"

"Hunh? Lance is here."

"Hey, hi Felicity," waved Lance, as he returned from the litter box. "I'm sorry I didn't tell you about the secret project. Your father asked me not to."

"I don't understand…?"

Claude bowed his head. "I'm so ashamed. I'm a sorry excuse for a cat. I'm supposed to be a carnivore, prey-driven, a consumer of meat, yet here I am chopping beets for their red juices and mixing them into my impawsible burgers, soysages and other deli-lites. And to make matters worse, I brought your beloved into this sham ham business. I'm so sorry."

Felicity stared at her father in disbelief. "But what about Chuck? Stu? Good ol' sloppy Joe?"

"Oh, I thought I mentioned it to you earlier, honey. They've moved on and are now managing DeliCatLondon, DeliCatParis and DeliCatJerseyCity respectively. And if Lance here is the bit of fresh meat I believe he is, the two of you may soon manage a DeliCat of your own."

A Model Murder
by Z.B. Wagman

The victim was skinny. Too skinny. Detective Sarah hated seeing it. And it was a sight she had gotten used to. These girls with their bottle-blonde hair, legs the size of twigs, probably wanted to be a model. A life of glitz and glam. Probably met a boy and ended up here: at the bottom of the stairs. Shoes missing and head on backwards.

Sarah tore her gaze away from the body. It wasn't her job to clean up this mess. But she could find the one responsible. The crime scene was bereft of any obvious clues. No bloody handprints or last words scratched into the wall by the victim. In fact, the walls were almost too clean.

Sarah ran a finger along the wall closest to the victim. She could just make out the faint shadow of felt tip--some long forgotten graffiti. But when she sniffed her finger there was the familiar scent of bleach. No fingerprints would be found here.

There was something about this scene that bugged her. She glanced back at the body. Light glistened off its face, too plastic to be alive. What was wrong with this picture? Aside from the backwards head. Something was missing…She closed her eyes, running through the crime scene in her mind. The missing pumps. The broken neck. The body sprawled at the foot of the stairs.

Her eyes shot open as she sprinted up the stairs, her heart pounding in time with her feet. As if to confirm her suspicion, a lone pink pump welcomed her at the top.

The hall infront of her was a short one. Only three doors branching off for three possible locations for a killer to hide. One stood half open, musty air wafting out from within. The second was closed tight and intimately familiar to Sarah. It was certainly safe. But the last…plastered with warning signs and toxic symbols, it was the perfect place for a killer to hide. As she crept up to it, she could see light playing at the foot of the door. She leaned down, ear to the crack.

"We shoulda kept the girl." It was the wheedly drawl of a born psycho.

"No way. There'd be too much trouble."

"Then at least we shoulda taken her clothes."

This was it for Sarah. Before she could think about consequences she was through the door, gun drawn. "Nobody move."

"Hey!" The two creeps sat on the floor, hunched over something Sarah couldn't see.

"Who did it?" Sarah could hear her voice rising. She couldn't help it. "Who killed the barbie?"

"Go away, Sarah," grunted the psycho one.

"Yeah," the warty one squawked. "We haven't touched your barbies."

But the words rang hollow as Sarah caught sight of the pink plastic pump that sat on the floor between them. Its heel had been melted into a sticky goo and singe marks licked its toe. Warty caught her eye and grinned. "It was just a little fun," he said, flicking the lighter in his hand.

"You monster." Sarah's voice was calmer than it had any right to be. She raised her pistol.

"You wouldn't dare," Psycho laughed.

Her first rubber band caught him right between the eyes.

The Barrel
by Holly Day

For as long as he could remember, the barrel had sat in the backyard, behind a locked gate and a very tall fence. Only the father had the key, and three times a day, the boy would watch his father take a jumbled plate of scraps out to the backyard to leave at the opening of the barrel, which was a large as a big dog's house and lay on its side, the opening facing away from the gate. The boy himself was not allowed in the backyard, but would accompany the father to the gate, which he would hold open to keep it from slamming shut with the father still inside, which would be a bad thing and wouldn't trap the father back there at all—only inconvenience him.

After the boy and the father were finished eating inside, quickly and without conversation, the father would go back out into the yard and return with a plate so empty and clean it was as though it had been swabbed with a gigantic floppy tongue. Sometimes the boy thought a big, messy dog must live inside the barrel, some ferocious beast too dangerous to live in the yard or the house like a regular dog, and sometimes he thought the barrel itself was the living thing with the big, floppy tongue, swabbing the bits of meat and potatoes from the plate like a mop swabbing the deck of a ship.

The boy had spent a lot of time trying to imagine what it looked like when the barrel ate the scraps brought to it on the old, chipped ceramic plate. Did a long, pink, sticky tongue come out and delicately lap food off the plate? Did some sort of hose protrude at mealtimes to suck the food off the surface of the plate, like a vacuum cleaner extension, or the way mouths of the tiny tank snails worked in the fish tank at the doctor's office? He could only imagine the answer, though, because his father would not let him step even one single step into the backyard when it was time to feed the barrel. "Not one step past the gate." He didn't dare ask his father if he could come out and feed the barrel with him. He didn't dare ask his father anything.

Sometimes, when the boy was outside playing, he'd think about the barrel. The barrel was in the backyard, and the boy was only allowed in the front. A giant wooden fence surrounded the backyard. It was too high for the boy to see over, but not so high that if his father was locked in the backyard, he couldn't escape. They'd talked about this many times. The only way into it or out of it was through the gate and through the back door of the house, both of which were always locked. The boy's father was the only one in the whole world with a key. "Stay out of the backyard," he'd say to the boy, any time he saw the boy looking at the big, locked door. "Don't even THINK about it," he said when he caught the boy trying to peep through a knothole in the tall wooden fence.

Once, the boy woke up in the middle of the night to a strange noise in the backyard. He got out of bed and went to the window. He could see the father in the backyard, hunched over next to the barrel, his lips moving. The boy couldn't tell what the father was saying, and he knew better than to open the window to hear better because he was to "NEVER open this window." It sounded like the barrel was crying. He couldn't tell what the father was saying, but it sounded like the barrel was crying. After a while, the father stood up. He patted the barrel awkwardly, like one would a dog or a small dragon, and marched briskly back to the house.

Before this incident, and afterwards, the boy spent the long, empty hours of the day wondering about the barrel. He drew pictures of the barrel and wrote stories on the backs of scratch paper about going to the backyard and making friends with the barrel. He was too little to go to school, and had no other children to play with, so his imaginary friendship with the barrel was his only friendship. When he played in the front yard, he would sometimes talk to the barrel through the tall wooden fence, but quietly, so the father, who was inside the house, couldn't hear him, and sometimes, when he went to bed at night, he would talk to the barrel through the window before drifting off to sleep.

One day, the father caught the boy drawing pictures of himself and the barrel playing together. In the picture, the boy was pushing the old wooden barrel on the rusty swing in the front yard. A long, slippery red tongue lolled out of a hole at one end, surrounded by a ring of sharp, white teeth. The father's face grew red and angry as he looked at the picture. The boy shrank into his chair, confused and frightened. The father was always angry, but there were different degrees to his anger that the boy was too young to have completely deciphered, each of which demanded a specific reaction. The boy did not understand why the picture made the father so angry.

"Stay away from that barrel!" the father finally shouted. He crumpled up the picture and threw it in the garbage. "Don't even THINK about the barrel!"

But the barrel was all the boy could think about. He would lie awake in bed long after the father put him in his room for the night and waited for the house to go quiet. As soon as he was sure the father was asleep, the boy would carefully tiptoe across the creaky wooden floor to look out the window at the barrel in the backyard. If he put his ear to the glass, he was sure he could hear the barrel singing, or crying, or making wet, blubbery, nonsense sounds to itself. Sometimes, the barrel would suddenly jerk and rock in place as though trying to roll away.

During the day, the boy tried his best to not think about the barrel. He tried to make up new imaginary friends to play with in the front yard, mostly other children like himself, sometimes fanciful talking animals. He'd give them all conspicuously manly names like "Tom," and "Peter," and "Randall," as the father seemed especially pleased with the boy when his imaginary friends had boy names. When he drew pictures of his imaginary friends, he made them all little boys like him, although, not having seen any other children except those in the books on the little shelf in his room, he often drew them with purple skin and green or pink hair. The father would frown slightly at these pictures, but since he didn't actually say anything, the boy went on drawing his imaginary friends in rainbow hues.

Nighttime dedicated to imaginings about the barrel. In his dreams, the barrel sprouted legs and arms and could run about the yard like a person, or on all fours like a dog. When it was on all fours, it sprouted a long, wet tongue like a dog, and panted, and drooled, and barked. When it was on two legs, it laughed, and shouted, and said nice things to the boy, like, "You're my best friend," or, "Do you want to run away with me?"

The dreams were so alluring to the boy that he began to think of ways to make them come true. The window in his bedroom had been nailed shut for as long as he could remember, but he could see how easy it would be to take the nails out. Every night, after the father went to bed, the boy carefully dug at the soft pine windowsill in his room with the tines of a fork, and slowly, over the course of many nights, the nails began to come out. He was so careful not to make any noise. He was careful not to scratch the glass. He was careful not to leave scratches on the frame with the fork. And most careful of all, whenever he pulled a nail out, he pushed it back into the hole and pulled it out again, until the hole was compromised just enough that the nail would slip out with a gentle tug. A casual visual inspection would leave one with the opinion that all of the nails were in place and the window was still secure.

When all the nails had finally been loosened, the boy scarcely dared to push the window upwards. When he finally did, the ancient wood frame gave a terrible, loud screech. The boy stopped and carefully, quietly, pushed the window shut and jumped into bed. A few seconds later, the door to his room opened and the father's silhouette filled the doorway. "Was that you?" The boy kept silent, eyes tightly closed, unmoving in his bed. After a few seconds, the father turned away and shut the door behind him.

As soon as he was gone, the boy quietly crept out of bed and went back to the window. This time, the pane slid up easily, silently. The window gaped open to the backyard. The barrel loomed in its corner of the yard.

The boy squeezed out the window and tiptoed across the yard. He could see the father sitting at the kitchen table through the small window in the back door, an open beer bottle in one hand, his attention focused on the newspaper spread out on the table before him. The boy had always assumed the two of them went to sleep at exactly the same time. He hadn't anticipated the father being in the kitchen, a full view of the backyard right beside him. He just had to turn his head. The boy almost went back in the house right there, but then the barrel gave a little jerk, as if trying to signal him.

The boy took a deep breath and ran as fast as he could to the barrel. Any minute, the father would turn around and see him. He would reach the barrel before the father turned around. It was so close. And then he was there.

"Hello?" the boy whispered. He dropped to his knees and peered inside the dark of the barrel, into the opening faced away from his bedroom window and the gate in the fence, the side he had never been able to see clearly. It was so much larger up close than it had appeared from the kitchen, from his bedroom, from where he obediently waited for his father at the gate. It was almost as big around as he was tall. He could see something moving inside, something way in back. He crept closer, until his head was almost inside the barrel. "Hello?"

Long, thin arms reached out and grabbed the boy. He squeaked and squirmed and tried to get away as the arms pulled him completely into the barrel. Pendulous breasts and long, matted hair brushed his skin. Thin arms pulled him close to a body that smelled horrible yet so familiar.

"Shhh," whispered a voice near his ear. "Shhh, baby. Shhh. Mine, mine, all mine," the voice began to softly sing. The body rocked back and forth, clutching the boy tightly, rocking him, too. "Mine, mine, all mine. You're all mine now."

The boy began to cry. He wanted out. He wanted back in his bed, the safety of his room. He wanted the father to come and get him, to rescue him from the stinky darkness of the barrel.

"Don't cry, little one," cooed the voice, still rocking, one hand over his mouth. Fingers combed through the boy's hair, brushing it back from his forehead. "Don't cry. Someone will feed us soon."

Ode to the Manifesto Written on a Chrysler Pacifica in a Barnes and Noble Parking Lot

by Lindsay Granduke

I am Saturn, serpent god
      Metallica, Brightburn, Fury
sonshine must be exalted
      holy holy holy

masked = 6, Master = 6
      monkey / wrench / system = 666
(they tell us to believe in Superman, that a country bumpkin)
      (could never hurt us, when he could easily take the world)

(and there would be no one who could stop him)
      police / sirens / klaxon – all of them 6
it adds up; but we keep rolling, to strike
      when the embers are hot. we must, or face destruction

idiocracy = a *(that Cohen film in 2006)*
      (where a soldier wakes up in a world intellectually stagnant)
(I'm starting to see the patterns)
      (were you in hibernation? are we?)

(will my Google history get sicked)
      (on me like a drug hound sniffing)
(for 24 kilobytes of crazy?)
      (maybe they're onto something)

(and if you are, tell H.P. Lovecraft to give me back my stars)

Exchanged
by Lynette G. Esposito

It was just before sunset every twenty-four hours to the second. She appeared, whispered one word; then was gone. I stood on the hill behind the house for fifteen years just before twilight at that exact same time trying to hear the word.

Every time, a bird chirped, a truck rumbled, it thundered, or something. I heard a start of a word like "Ka". Over and over I heard the same thing. KA Ka Ka ...like a crow or hawk or dolphin.

If you take 365 days times 15 years, you have one big number. I figured one day I will hear the full word and know what to do.

The sun made a half smile on the horizon so I figured I would stand on the hill in total silence and concentrate. If I could not decipher the word this time, I would stop. I would give up trying to get the woman I loved back in my life. Of course, I've had this same argument with myself before.

The time was here again. I downed one more shot and got up too quick and knocked the whiskey bottle to the floor. Visions of my beautiful Sophia at sunset flashed before my eyes as I scrambled for the bottle so it wouldn't spill. I carefully twisted the cap, set it back on the table and ran to get the woman I loved back into my life.

The sun was sinking. Shocked, I stood in disbelief. Fifteen years and now this.

"Ka" I heard from a distance.

I'm here I shouted. Right here. I'm coming. My feet didn't follow my command and suddenly I am rolling down the hill instead of running up it. I lay there on the wet grass. She called. I thought I heard her but I knew it was too late. My shirt was smeared with dirt and I thought I pulled a hamstring. The left leg buckled under me and my knee hit a stone as I went down. This day was turning out to be one of the worst I ever had.

"Ka. Ka, Ka."

I trudged up the hill. Fifteen years, loyal, loving, trying to figure out the word to break the alien's code all for nothing.

But there she stood. My wife. Human, in the flesh. She hadn't aged.

"Katcho."

Kunzite, I said. These were our first words after so long.

"I've been trying to sneeze for such a long time. When you weren't here, it finally happened. It is so different in a space ship. I was paralyzed by fear. They kept watching me waiting for me to do something but I couldn't."

I hollered What?

"They kept watching you come back over and over. I kept watching you hoping you could save me."

Where are they now I asked wanting to embrace this young wife in my older arms.

"Dunno," she said and skipped down the hill as if nothing had happened.

It struck me. I was inside the space ship. "Ka."

The Art of Detection
by Kate Falvey

The ideal woman is
very brightly colored.
She is shiny; her breasts
point in sharp
conical assertion of
their amazing defiance of
physical laws; her waist
turns where she leans or
backs away and, if
she is clothed her
static swiveling rumples
her neat skirt, shifting and
hitching it over her
neat hips. Her lap
seems emphasized. Her legs
always exert themselves.
If she is clothed, her leg
is outlined in the creased
folds of her
twisting. Some of it,
usually her thigh, obtrudes
where her skirt is
torn or hefted.

She comes in three
colors and three
expressions.

If she is black, she is
white. Darkness goes
with earring size. Loops
of long gold go with
bare shoulders and,
in general, more
skin which goes with
darkness. If she is
Oriental she is not

white but she is
only one kind of
Oriental and her sloe
eyes crouch, watching
in deep blue lashes.
If she is white she is
a secretary and her short
hair curls in a damp
controlled sheen onto her straining
neck. She can be
aghast and terrified; appalled and
horrified; or icy and amused at some
awful private knowing.

There may be another
way she looks though it
doesn't show itself
often. She
might look a touch
weary, as if she
were holding her arms
before her breasts and
stopping a something
from coming for
way too
long.

She costs thirty-five cents.
My father buys her all the time.

II

Give me a female sleuth any day,
whether she is matronly and nosy,
the kind of overlooked aunt who
fades into the marmalade, outshone by
a gleam of fresh butter on the toast,
given to meddling and shapelessness,
sprightly in her garden, shipshape among
the crockery and creamware, all
taken-for-granted tweeds and grey and navy
worsted wools and serviceable walking shoes

and greeting the twice-a-day postman
and prickling the humorless village vicar
and seeing to it that
evil
even in the midland counties
is rousted,
stared gravely down, and
ingeniously
traduced
or
whether she is importunate in suave
efficiency, disciplined, tall, fetching
in insouciant glamor, every molecule poised
for success and intricate, dignified capers,
intelligence like a clear bell sounding in an island fog,
emerging from any mayhem with stratagems intact and
scrying the titian glow in the snifter
or rousing a tinkle of ice in the moody old scotch,
drifting into a heady rhapsody of planning and outwitting,
and measured, attentive, lusty competence,
assuring that
if the needle lurks in the haystack still
it will point itself for plucking,
the perverse compass of its ornery
pathology insisting on being known,
and then, even if she is herself
bane and bait, she
steels her nautical, New England nerves
and makes visible
and fellable
the artfulness of
monsters

or
whether she is insolent and cussed,
acrimonious and solo, favoring
greasy meals and dark ales with showy heads
in derelict saloons with juke tunes gunning
and the seen-it-all barkeep scanning with
fatherly watchfulness, her
handicap of temper which spurs her to sudden lurches
of ill-judgment and enriches the mystery with her
scrabbling in and out of scrapes, and, smart-

mouthed, mightily self-sufficient,
boot to the floor of her coupe as she blares
like a suspect fire through the Sausalito canyons,
a hot date with trouble and ready for it, able
to get ferociously angry and,
cunning in her own imprecise way,
she maneuvers doggedly, near-fearlessly through
the minds of whackos and bludgeoners and gets
right into the cracks where the demons force
their lava and then she stuns them
without pity
when they sleep.

III.

This is something I
think about often.

Someone takes away
your place in line
and it is because
their own indignation
is unappeasable and they
can be faulted but
understood to be
aggressively sad and so
pity is warranted, at least
adulterated with annoyed
antipathy, but reprisals
must be tame, a look or a
mild dressing down or a stuffy
reminder that manners
and other lives
matter, or else,
even if your look is too
withering, your tone too
sanctimonious, your sense of
infringement too particular and
pronounced, and even if you
do nothing else,
suffer restraint and check
outrage with memories of
mercy, and

not even utter a caution or
aggrieved resistance or
defense, you
risk, still,
noticing that
you are no better
than they.

And this happens
every day.

IV.

A child is running
and there are no
doorways.

Love Languages
by Nicole Chvatal

My mom's is easy: She tells me I look pretty.

My lipstick's love for me runs so deep I ingest a pound per year.

My brother drives a stick shift and brings me lobster
he caught earlier. He soaks the clams for an extra hour
to clean out any excess grit.

Dorner handwrites letters and her texts include
the emojis I forget about: Peacock, air mail, fleur-de-lis.

My favorite jeans hold me in shape of me.

It's my dad who is the challenge.
His love language is a binary code,
a cracked Rosetta Stone.
If my dad were an emoji, he would be the face of a slot
machine, withholding funds before bumming a smoke.
I am half of him—the nose, auburn hair,
the sad parts hidden in the middle.
The last time he called, it was something about
the importance of an upgrade
to my iOS, and was I backing up to the cloud,
and did I know the ease of wireless chargers vs. the coiled cord.
When he offered recently to buy me a new phone
his text startled me awake. Must have forgotten
the three-hour time difference between us.
Half asleep, I could barely see the screen.

for
by Mark D Cart

there's a film
over everything
we've had our fill--
fed and fattened up
on but still lift
heavenward
as we file into
that afterlife

& whether
fussed over
or laughed at
be treated
as artfully
and outdated
as the dead allow
suffered yet
again

The Mole People
by Mickey Collins

I never thought that a mole people invasion would happen in my lifetime.

They had always been there, waiting. We don't know why, they just were. And then one day, they broke through the surface. Out of the blue. I had heard stories of it happening to cities far away from ours, but our town was quiet, it was peaceful. When we--my wife and I--heard the news, I cried. Surely this would be a significant change to our lifestyles.

To begin with, one is never to make eye contact with a mole person. It was said that they could invade your mind, make you one of them. And then you would spend the rest of your days digging holes for the Mole Queen. One should black out the windows with newspaper and cardboard. Therefore we were kept in the dark, quite literally, about the goings on of the outside world during that time. All we could do was listen to the weekly newscast on how things were progressing. They had illustrations of what an imagined mole person could look like, though no one could know for sure.

We had prepared, like our neighbors, for this eventuality, but we never thought that we would actually have to use our "in case of mole people" emergency stores. We had joked about it (ha), that mole people invasions weren't that common and moles weren't that scary. My wife would point to a mole on her arm, "Am I a mole person? Watch out!" We laughed.

The mayor seemed confident at the beginning. It was a small invasion, easy to remove, they said. So long as they don't pop up anywhere else they'll eventually be done away with. The police used a mixture of poison and explosives, sometimes in deterrence, other times with intent to kill.

Our eyes adjusted to the dark. We ate when we felt hungry and scrounged around our piles of food and supplies. We played games at the beginning by candlelight. Near the end of the two weeks I began to pace around the living room, creating a pathway through debris and clothes. At times I felt like I was becoming a mole. I felt nauseous more days than not.

I would lay awake at night, early in the invasion, listening for any sounds that would update me on the state of the world. I would imagine the screams of moles, distant dynamite exploding underground, but nothing ever came close enough to make a difference. I was always left wondering what would happen tomorrow. What if the mole people stormed the mayor's office? What if they replaced our doctors, our police, our teachers with mole versions? Could we ever really feel safe again?

The mayor gave us a timeline of two weeks. That's all it would take for this to blow over. Stay inside, hunker down, keep your windows blacked out.

The mayor's two week prediction became ten weeks. We're close, he said. We've isolated their hiding hole. It's just a matter of time.

And so we waited while the police fought the moles and the doctors and nurses tended to the wounded, we waited and prayed.

One day, it was just over. The mayor announced that the moles had been fought back successfully. He reminded us to restock on emergency mole supplies. You never know when they'll return. They'll always be just under the surface. Somewhere. They could reappear in another town, could even relapse here if we weren't careful. But of course there's nothing you can do.

We ripped off the cardboard from our windows. We saw the bright sunshine upon our town once more. There were holes polka dotted down our street either from the moles or the dynamite. It didn't matter.

There were already people filling the holes back in with piles of gravel and dirt.

I looked at my wife, smiling in the sun. She was wan. We both were.

"Watch out," she said. "I think the mole on my arm got bigger!" She leapt at me in an embrace.

FLY BOTTLE
by Jonathan van Belle

To whom it may concern,

I recently purchased your PSC03R-050 2.5 watt USB adapter with interchangeable plugs. Your output specifications indicated that the PSC03R-050 had a maximum load of 0.5A. I tested my unit and I found that your specification was untrue in my case. I do not wish for a refund. I am informing you so that your company may improve its quality control.

Regards,
Hermann Rorty
155 Elmira Loop
Apartment #110
Brooklyn, NY 11239

I finished my letter at 2:51am on the 21st of August 2009. 72° Fahrenheit outside. Precipitation was nearly 11%.

"In October of 1978, Idi Amin invaded Tanzania" whispered through the custom, herringbone-design radio grill cloth of my Sangean retro-style AM/FM radio.

I noted these "coincident details," as I call them, details about the precipitation and the historical program on my radio, in my yellow, spiral-bound Caliber notebook, on whose face I had, two weeks previous, drawn two symbols: a Fourchée cross and the Assyrian cuneiform character for "field." The Fourchée cross occupied the center of the yellow cover and the Assyrian cuneiform character occupied the lower left-hand side of the yellow Caliber cover. My reasons for adding these flourishes were as follows: The Fourchée cross signified—for reasons I won't list—my father, Jacob Turner Rorty, born in Bedford-Stuyvesant on April 2nd, 1949 at 4:22pm. The Assyrian cuneiform character for "field" signified—also for reasons I won't enumerate—my favorite planetary satellite: the Mimas co-orbital (my second favorite planetary satellite is the Dione co-orbital).

This notebook was the 59th such notebook in my archive of yellow, spiral-bound Caliber notebooks. Each notebook received its own special title, written on the first page and chosen for any number of reasons. This 59th notebook I had titled *Satyricon*—a choice made nearly inevitable by the fact that 59 B.C.E. is the most probable date for the creation of Petronius's Satyricon.

Notebook #58 was titled *NASA*, on account of the founding of the National Aeronautics and Space Administration in 1958. Notebook #57 was titled *Glinka*, for the Russian composer Mikhail Glinka, who died in 1857. Notebook #56 was titled *Barium*, on account of the fact that the atomic number for the element barium is 56. Notebook #55 was titled *Zero*—for five minus five. And so on, all the way back to Notebook #1, *Monic Polynomial*.

Examining my latest entry, I noticed that I had filled up the front side of the negative twenty-first page of *Satyricon*. [As a clarification, I do not number a single page with two numbers—one number for the back and one number for the front of a single sheet. Instead, I identify a single sheet of paper with a single number, where each number counts back into the negatives of the whole numbers, and skipping even numbers; e.g. -1, -3, -5, -7, and so on.] I flipped to the backside of page negative twenty-one and made the following entry:

The information on the other side of this same page refers to events occurring on a date (August 21st, 2009) that corresponds to the numerical identification of the page on which that information is written.

Initial Associations:

[August]: Eighth month of the year in Julian and Gregorian calendars; Augustus Caesar; St. Augustine; Augury; AU = symbol for gold; August 1983, Prime Minister Sankara overthrows Ouédrago; August 1998, I met Cynthia Sprent, receptionist at West Heights Dental; etc.

[21]: Blackjack; Gustave Flaubert born 1821; XXI in Roman numeral system; 21 is a Fibonacci number; Age of father, Jacob Turner Rorty, when I was born; current century is the 21st century; 21 grams is the weight of the soul, according to research by Duncan MacDougall; etc.

Cross-Pollinations:

(A) Book XXI of St. Augustine's *City of God* is divided into 27 chapters. The 21st chapter of Book XXI begins "The belief that all who hold the Catholic faith are to be saved, however evil their lives." Gold is mentioned in chapter 21 of Book XXI: "For if anyone builds on that foundation in gold, silver, precious stones, or in timber, hay, or straw, the work done by each man will be revealed." St. Augustine is here quoting from 1 Corinthians 3:12-13. Question: What is the probability that the 21st chapter of Book XXI of St. Augustine's *City of God* would mention an item, gold, that is independently included in my Initial Associations?

It was 3:41am when I finished this last entry. I closed *Satyricon*, walked to my bookcase, closed my eyes, reached out my hand, and grabbed at random for a book. I opened my eyes and found *The Wordsworth Dictionary of Classical and Literary Allusion* (ed. 1994) in my hands. I sat down on my 1952 Diamond model Harry Bertoia chair and I flipped at random and stopped at random on some page of the dictionary. My eyes still closed, I scrolled my index finger up and down and up and down the page. I then stopped my finger.

Page 181, "Priscilla."

Priscilla. In the narrative poem, *The Courtship of Miles Standish* (1858), by Henry Wordsworth Longfellow, the Pilgrim captain Miles Standish (see Standish, Miles) enlists the young scholar John Alden to press his suit to marry the orphaned Priscilla. Priscilla refuses Standish and tells Alden to "Speak for yourself, John." He does and the two are married.

I opened *Satyricon* and copied the above entry verbatim, right below the entry about August and 21. I made a small, bracketed note about how my random entry selection happened to mention Wordsworth and that the book in which I had made this random selection was titled *The Wordsworth Dictionary of Classical and Literary Allusion*.

I again closed *Satyricon*. I then returned the dictionary of allusions to its shelf (Shelf A9). I rotated the radio dial, until I heard: "The exact location of the geomagnetic poles is constantly changing." I settled onto my mattress with one cup of Kikkoman Pearl organic chocolate soymilk; 8 grams of protein, 180 milligrams of sodium, and 290 milligrams of potassium per 240mL.

I again rotated the radio dial, until I heard: "Stimulating the charge of body's polar opposites in order to heal." I was tempted to jot down the coincidence of polar references coming from the radio, but it was seven minutes after 4:00am, and 4:00am signified an end-of-transmission or an end-of-routine time. I stop all my work at 4:00am. 4:00am is my Sabbath hour.

4:00am was the hour that my mother and my father died. At 4:00am Monday morning, October 1st, 2007, Jacob Turner Rorty and Patricia May Rorty were killed by a collision with a yellow 2006 Freightliner CST12064-Century 120 diesel truck, 10-speed transmission, 239-inch wheelbase, engine horsepower 515, front axle weight of 12,000 pounds, rear axle weight of 40,000 pounds. The collision occurred on New Jersey State Highway Route 440, near Woodbridge Township.

I fell asleep sometime after 4:27am, still buzzing inside with correlations, bits of news, names, holidays, unsorted sequences of shapes, visions of dishware, measurements, mysteries, and a memory of a bodega on East 28th Street and Avenue U.

Flocci Volitantes: A Metaphysical Mystery

by Yuan Changming

Drifting like broken shadows

Are the floaters illusionary
Fragments of last night
Or shredded shadows
Of my own protobeing?

How often am I tempted
To catch one of them
With my inner hands!

History of Knotted Artifacts
by Mike Corrao

Years of Settlement

yoS 1 → Dhagren births two gallstones and plants them in the planet's corrupted soil. The gallstones grow into radiant objects [a sword hilt & a melted ribcage]. Dhagren adorns their body, placing the former on their hip and the latter over their chest. The fusion emits a psionic radiation.

yoS 1 → A primordial terraphage consumes the landscape and mutates every eco-system.

yoS 31 → Small settlements begin forming in biologically compliant biomes [taiga-desert, deciduous-forest-tundra, freshwater-grasslands].

yoS 53 → The Malady Church is formed by a group of nomadic priests led by Geresh Symth, Kei-Man Ra, and Ihy-Yett Yanak.

yoS 58 → The city of Under Reef is established in the deciduous-forest-tundra.

yoS 59 → The Malady Church publishes a doctrine outlining the tenants of their order. Foundational passages detail an ancient plague and its role in creating the first sentient beings.

yoS 62 → Under Reef's university is founded by Dhagril Yan, mainly focused on studies of the occult and the astral.

yoS 71 → The sword hilt and melted ribcage become permanently sutured to Dhagren's body. The consciousness of the artifacts and their bearer become indistinguishable.

yoS 75 → Small settlements begin forming in biologically non-compliant biomes [tundra-desert, arctic-savanna, chaparral-grasslands].

yoS 75 → Dhagril Yan discovers the existence of the Negative

Material Plane (NMP), an astral landscape severed from our reality.

Years of Anticipation

yoA 1 → Senior faculty from The University of Under Reef perform their first expedition into the NMP, observing for the first time, its esoteric ecosystems and non-euclidean geology.

yoA 1 → Key participants [Ous'Elkt Pagac & De'Iah Mormil] research botanical samples brought back from the NMP and find that, upon consumption, they may grant the subject psionic properties.

yoA 10 → Dhagren establishes a small settlement in the tundra-desert biome, cut off from neighboring city-states.

yoA 15 → Ous'Elkt Pagac & De'Iah Mormil synthesize a salve from the NMP's botanical samples. The salve is hypothesized to briefly grant its user clairvoyance.

yoA 18 → Under Reef's university creates a Department of Negative Planar Botany.

yoA 25 → Farmland settlements to the north of Under Reef begin reporting anomalous events [necroluminsence, stone rain, mutated crops].

yoA 26 → Etherea is established in the freshwater-grasslands biome.

yoA 36 → Noncanonical texts begin to appear in the Malady Church, depicting the ancient plague as a *flame sickness* [interior bodily combustion] conjured by the mancer, Ignus. The author of these texts is unknown.

yoA 40 → Two new artifacts appear in the deciduous-forest-tundra biome [stone mandible & mirrored sphere]. Under Reef archaeologists bring them back to the university and study their properties. Similar to the NMP botanical samples, they emit a psionic radiation, although the application of this radiation remains unknown.

yoA 45 → The Department of Negative Planar Botany creates a more stable form of interplanar travel. The production of the NMP salve [Deridance] drastically increases.

yoA 46 → Ous'Elkt Pagac & De'Iah Mormil establish themselves as powerful clairvoyants through excessive use of deridance. They become powerful members of the university's council.

yoA 57 → A group of ornithomancers instigate the formation of a new artifact [ibis skull] during a seemingly innocuous feather scrying ritual.

yoA 60 → Dhagren teaches themself how to detect the appearance of new artifacts using energy siphoned from the NMP. They soon depart from the tundra-desert biome.

yoA 60 → Dhagren acquires the stone mandible & mirrored sphere from Under Reef's university and sutures them to their body [the means of this acquisition is not recorded].

yoA 73 → Etherea issues a small-scale investigation of the anomalous activities occurring in the farmland settlements.

yoA 75 → Dhagren acquires the ibis skull through violent means.

Years of Hunger

yoH 1 → The Malady Church is beheaded. Two prominent members [Aza'Imp Headroun & Aze'Iah Akkadum] depart and create the Order of Self-Capture & the Order of Small Fires respectively.

yoH 1 → The Order of Self-Capture establishes a base of operations in the vast catacombs beneath the Malady Church.

yoH 1 → Ous'Elkt Pagac dies of an unnatural illness. De'Iah Mormil hypothesizes that it is due to deridance withdrawal, and drastically increases his use of the salve.

yoH 3 → The Order of Small Fires migrates to Etherea and begins construction of an ornate cathedral.

yoH 3 → De'Iah Mormil departs from the Department of Negative Planar Botany.

yoH 5 → De'Iah Mormil becomes a messianic figure and soon amasses a small following. Fearing his shrinking supply of deridance, De'Iah Mormil steals the university's distillation instruments, and leads his followers into the NMP.

yoH 5 → Under Reef's university temporarily seals all access to the NMP and makes the remaining supply of deridance available for public consumption.

yoH 12 → Large swaths of the Under Reef population become addicted to the salve, but due to limited supply, quickly begin to suffer withdrawal symptoms [discoloration of the eyes, dental decay, large calluses on the chest and abdomen].

yoH 14 → Anomalous activity in the farmland settlements drastically increases. Etherea expands their investigation and creates the Astral Research Body [ARB] to oversee progress.

yoH 18 → Fearing the degradation of their memories, Dhagren creates the Tome of Collectamancy, articulating everything they know of the artifacts and their supranatural qualities. Included is a detailed procedure for suturing these artifacts to the subject's body.

yoH 18 → Dhagren gifts the tome to their followers and departs to work in isolation in the peripheries of the tundra-desert biome.

yoH 23 → The farmland settlements suffer an unforgiving drought. Under Reef, Etherea, and the Malady Church all experience widespread famine.

yoH 24 → The Order of Small Fires quickly become the dominant religious body in Etherea.

yoH 30 → The Department of Negative Planar Botany is greatly reduced in order to reallocate resources to departments studying alternative agriculture practices.

yoH 34 → Under Reef begins experiments in nematode farming.

yoH 37 → De'Iah Mormil dies of deridance withdrawal in the NMP. His followers attempt to re-establish connection with Under Reef.

yoH 38 → Sau Gaet invents a sustainable system for nematode farming.

yoH 40 → The farmland settlements begin to recover after the devastation of the drought. Large scale nematode farms are constructed across the region.

yoH 52 → Etherea's ARB concludes that the anomalous activities in the farmland settlements are a result of psionic radiation from the NMP. Under Reef's university is accused of committing crimes against all sentient beings.

yoH 53 → The heirs of Ous'Elkt Pagac & De'Iah Mormil [Ous'Elkt Ittre & De'Iah Valek respectively] are arrested. In an Etherean court, the heirs are sentenced to exile.

yoH 55 → Ous'Elkt Ittre & De'Iah Valek are publicly banished into the NMP.

yoH 57 → Ous'Elkt Ittre & De'Iah Valek find a small colony run of Ous'Elkt Pagac's followers, who have created rudimentary techniques for synthesizing deridance.

yoH 63 → Dhagren continues to revise the Tome of Collectamancy, studying the changes in their condition as they collect and synthesize new artifacts in the biologically non-compliant biomes. Each new object is sutured onto Dhagren's frame. And in turn, Dhagren continues to grow in size.

yoH 71 → De'Iah Valek dies in the NMP's inhospitable environment. Ous'Elkt Ittre gains the favor of her father's followers and establishes herself as the reincarnation of Ous'Elkt Pagac. The colony begins to experiment with interplanar travel.

yoH 75 → Eyon'Rada Panorm of the Malady Church, under the influence of deridance, prophesizes the onset of another great plague.

yoH 75 → Dhagren's long-term memory suffers major

deterioration.

Years of Reincarnation

yoR 1 → Ous'Elkt Ittre and her followers return from the NMP with a caravan of deridance and found the city-state of Cit-Pagac in the freshwater-grasslands biome.

yoR 2 → In response to Ous'Elkt Ittre's return, Etherea systemically severs all known entrances to the NMP.

yoR 7 → Ous'Elkt Ittre creates the Treatise of Reparation, demanding that Etherea answer for its wrongful sentencing and dismantle their hereditary laws.

yoR 10 → Cit-Pagac and Etherea are unable to reach an agreement. Cit-Pagac declares war.

yoR 12 → The Malady Church, anticipating another great plague, begins experiments to synthesize new artifacts for the church's protection.

yoR 14 → Cit-Pagac burns all major nematode farms, disrupting food supplies to Under Reef and Etherea.

yoR 15 → Eyon'Rada Panorm creates three new artifacts [mucoused rag, broken vial, & severed callous] and attempts to suture them to his body. The procedure is unsuccessful.

yoR 15 → Etherea suffers major casualties in the war against Cit-Pagac.

yoR 15 → Under Reef experiments with new subterranean agricultural practices. The population feeds on the byproducts of these tests, leading to minor disease cycles, and an increased mortality rate.

yoR 18 → Dhagren is drawn from their hermitage by the emission of new artifacts and begins their migration towards the Malady Church.

yoR 19 → Etherea is sieged by Ous'Elkt Ittre.

yoR 20 → Etherea falls and is absorbed into the Pagacan Domain. Former leaders and court officials are publicly executed.

yoR 26 → Without access to the NMP, the supply of deridance quickly dwindles. The remaining stock is reserved for Ous'Elkt Ittre and her original followers.

yoR 32 → The Order of Self-Capture emerges from the Malady Church catacombs demanding control of the surface structure. A bloody confrontation leads to the death of Eyon'Rada Panorm and the seizure of his artifacts. The Order of Self-Capture begins altering prominent holy texts.

yoR 33 → Transcriptions of the Tome of Collectamancy become widespread, eventually making their way to the University of Under Reef.

yoR 37 → Ous'Elkt Ittre dies of natural causes without an heir. The Pagacan Domain falls into civil war. Two factions emerge: The Apostles of Ous'Elkt Ittre [led by her original followers] and The Order of Small Fires [led by Griet Al'Tuler].

yoR 37 → The Order of Small Fires spreads doctrine detailing the oncoming annihilation throughout the Pagacan Domain, warning of Ignus' return.

yoR 39 → Losing favor amongst the population, the Order of Small Fires unsuccessfully attempts to summon Ignus, instead creating a new artifact [charred wooden cube] which is seized by the Apostles.

yoR 39 → The Order of Small Fires is dismantled and its leaders are exiled by the Apostles of Ous'Elkt Ittre.

yoR 40 → Dhagren arrives in Cit-Pagac, now a lumbering mass of disparate artifacts. They ask for an audience with the Apostles, and out of intrigue, are granted one. Dhagren asks for the charred wooden cube. Seeing this as a treasonous request, the Apostles call for Dhagren's execution.

yoR 41 → Dhagren is unsuccessfully executed in the center of Cit-Pagac.

yoR 41 → The gallows fuse to Dhagren's body, expanding the collectamancer into an even larger being. In the public square, Dhagren demands the Apostles release the charred wooden cube into their custody.

yoR 41 → Dhagren quickly becomes a divine figure in the public eye and, fearing another period of unrest, the Apostles are forced to fulfill the collectamancer's demand.

yoR 41 → Dhagren departs for the Malady Church.

yoR 42 → Under Reef improves the infrastructure of their subterranean nematode farms, creating a sustainable food source within the confines of the city.

yoR 43 → Dhagren arrives at the Malady Church.

yoR 43 → Upon arrival, the Order of Self-Capture gifts Dhagren the three artifacts which they have inherited from Eyon'Rada Panorm. After suturing the mucoused rag, broken vial, and severed callous to their body, the collectamancer grows more immense than the church itself, now unable to leave its interior.

yoR 44 → The Order of Self-Capture worships Dhagren as a reincarnation of the ancient plague and renames themselves as the Collectamantic Order. They transcribe new editions of Dhagren's Tome, incorporating facets of the Malady Church's previous doctrine.

yoR 59 → Dhagren's long-term memory fully deteriorates, slowly turning the collectamancer into an instinctual organism, feeding themself only on the underlying desires of their brain [*What can change the nature of a man?*].

yoR 62 → Dhagren sutures the bodies of the Collectamantic Order to their ever-expanding frame. Reunifying the identity of the church's many orders.

yoR Null → A new entrance to the NMP forms at the base of the Malady Church. Sensing the vast artifacts scattered within, Dhagren enters. The Malady Church disappears from existence.

The Ghost in the Attic Closet
by Charles Halsted

As a five-year-old child, I was told I must never go near
the closet at the top of the attic stairs, where dwelled
a ghostly monster who survived on a diet of caterpillars,
spiders, and snails, but was known to devour children

so small they disappeared down its gullet with a single
swallow. Left behind by former owners, the ghost had
lived up there since the house was first built, before my
great-grandfather's return from the Civil War.

No matter what ritual I followed, such as climbing every
other stair or ascending each step on my hands and knees,
once I started to make my ascent, it would always know
which step I was on, ready to swallow me up at the top.

One day a boarder appeared, a new kindergarten teacher at my
school. My mother decided she would stay in our attic, arranged
for a bedroom to be built. For this to occur, the closet had to go.
The ghost flew off through the attic window, or so I was told.

The King's Man
by Ben Crowley

Three days since the great hall has been swept; three days since the mirrors, portraits and glass bowls draped in black; three days since the nightingales, choirs and trumpets were silenced; three days and the King still holds himself in a ball--no one has shaved him, no one has washed him.

The Knight of Forests and the Knight of Dragons take tiny gold spoons and force feed the King puddings, then push their hands on his mouth. The puddings squirm back through their fingers like red and white worms. The King, refusing all nourishment, refusing all light, refusing all sound, glows faintly in their candles, which he tries to blow out. His eyes burn like little coals. 'The prince, the prince, the prince, the prince, the prince,' is all the King will say.

Who has taken the prince? Who has kidnapped him? How many pieces is he in? It's all too hard for the King. Time has stopped for the King. The sun hasn't set for the king, but has only remained up above, totally still, hovering high like a sword over the Kingdom. If the sun won't go to bed, then neither will the king.

The Knight of Forests and the Knight of Dragons close the double doors and the King sits in the darkness of his throne, as if it were inside an egg. Somewhere else inside the castle, the only princess plays with dolls.

The King's man's only function was to know about the prince. He accompanied the prince on all his journeys, and joined in all the prince's leisure. Four feet tall, the King's man was the perfect shadow to the prince. If he did not find the prince, the King's man would be hanged. This was decreed. This, everybody knew.

The King's man walked down the hill from the castle to the barracks.

When he reached the great leather flap of the barracks, he took up the cudgel and knocked the steel plate. This was a place of great secrecy, the barracks. A massive tent with no windows and only a hole in the top. Smoke dribbled out day and night.

A bear emerged from the flap. He was not a bear, but a man. He glared at the sun. 'Who's there?' he said. He looked down. 'Ah, King's man,' he said, then pulled the little man in.

The inside was lit by other torches. Knights wrestled in various rings throughout the tent. At center, two knights wore black bags over their heads and wrestled naked. If they stepped out of the ring, they were pushed back in by other knights.

'I am in search of the prince,' said the King's man to the Bear Knight.

The Bear Knight nodded, escorting the King's man to a table with two older knights pushing little wooden horses around a map too big for the table.

'Who's that?' said the King's man.

Behind the men with the map, there was a tall wooden post. Tied to the post by his wrists was a young man. His face was swollen and he was covered in bruises.

'Don't pay any attention to him,' said the Bear Knight. 'Some villain we pulled out from the forest.'

The young man on the post, as if sensing the attention, bent his blue neck toward the King's man. His eyes were puffy like fruits. His hair, though discolored and dirty, was still somewhat blonde; his eyes glowed blue like hot springs; and his eyelashes sparkled like gold.

'You know,' said the Bear Knight. He was arranging two mugs to fill them with beer from a barrel on stilts. 'I'm glad you came to us first. We, the Knights Order, serve only the King.' He set the first beer full on the table, then took the second up. 'We know everything about the King. We kill who he wants, when he wants. But then who kills the King?'

Two flagons filled, the Bear Knight returned. One for himself and one for the King's man. They clinked and pulled in long gulps at foam.

'They've not killed the King,' said the King's man. 'They've just killed the prince.'

The Bear Knight shrugged and leaned back. 'Granted,' he said. 'The King is not dead. But now, who will carry his name? The princess?'

'Why not?'

'She's only seven-years old. The King's got what five years, six years? And now, after this assassination of the prince...'

'You're saying,' said the King's man. He leaned forward and spoke quieter. 'You're saying the Knights Order will not honor the princess after the death of the King?'

'I'm saying,' said the Bear Knight, shifting his elbows and leaning as close. 'I wouldn't count on that princess either.'

Both men were flushed red. They had finished their beers.

The King's man leaned back. 'I want to talk to that young man on the pole,' he said.

'He does not speak our language,' said the Bear Knight.

The King's man left the table and came to the young man tied to the post. 'Are you the prince?' he said.

The blue in the young man's crystal-blue eyes drifted slightly. He was not like a man in his nakedness. His body was raw. He writhed like a spider.

'Are you the prince?' said the King's man again.

The young man was suddenly splashed with a bucket of water, the Bear Knight behind it. The blonde hair became liquid. The dirt disappeared. The young man wiped his eyes with his wrists like a child. His hair and skin as white as an orchid, he opened his eyes. They were pink and not blue. He spoke three words in an unknown language, a language like rocks clacking and sliding.

'Why was he disguised?' said the King's man.

'I don't know,' said the Bear Knight.

'You're sure?'

'I have no idea.'

Throughout the knight's tent, men pinned each other in the various rings. There were screams of ecstasy, screams of pain and screams of commitment. The shadows of these men grew in the tent by the flames.

'If it is bodies you want, then go see the surgeons,' said the Bear Knight. 'We the Knights Order serve-'

'-only the King,' said the King's man.

The Bear Knight bowed royally and the men exchanged goodbyes. Then the Bear Knight turned back to the creature on the post.

As the King's man made his way to the leather flap, he passed the two blinded knights, still wrestling naked. They grunted and squeezed. One came from behind the other and hugged from his back. It seemed he would win, until the other lunged to his knees and his aggressor lifted off the ground, his torso stuck to the man's back, limbs struggling in the air like the legs of a crab.

The King's man pulled open the flap. There was the sun, a faint colorless lemon.

The King's man is a short man. He is a man of immense wit. He is blameless, and yet he is set to be hanged if he does not find the prince. *This is the way it is,* he thought. *To make us live well, we are threatened with death. I am to be hanged.*

The King's man walked down the hill to the barn.

The surgeons' barn was very different from the knights' barracks. It was full of free-flowing air, of windows and doors, so it seemed anyone could walk in or out. There was no theory of germs. This was not a precaution. It was only because they loved letting screams fly. The screams of surgery rang clear through the kingdom.

Outside on log benches, a number of surgeons rested against one wall of the barn. The conscious surgeons among them played a game throwing a leather-handled knife into a pumpkin. The King's man approached them.

'What'll it be?' said the one in the middle, after he sunk in the knife. 'I can't make you any more than a couple finger's-width taller.'

'I'm looking for the prince,' said the King's man.

The surgeon turned still. 'I wouldn't know anything about that,' he said.

'He's been missing three days,' said the King's man.

'That's too bad.' The surgeon led the King's man inside. They continued to talk, but were momentarily distracted. From a wooden tub near the barn entrance, two white arms splashed up screaming. The man's face was covered in leeches. He braced himself, gripping hard the edges of the tub. A number of surgeons rushed back over to force him back down.

'Look, if anyone asks, I know nothing.' The surgeon led the King's man to a man on a pile of straw. He was wrapped head to toe in white bandage. 'He came in yesterday morning. Nearly every bone broken.'

The man's eyes started through a slit in the bandage. They were as blue as hot springs, bordered by eyelashes that glittered like gold.

'This is the prince,' said the King's man.

'No,' said the surgeon. 'The eyes are the same. The hair is the same. But believe me.' He began shaking his head.

When the bandages over the young man's lips stirred, the King's man moved closer. The same incomprehensible language, like a very quiet landslide. However this time, as the King's man listened more closely: *That clacking*, he thought, *like something's hitting his teeth.*

'What language is that?' asked the King's man.

'It is the King's language,' said the surgeon. 'Only-' He rustled through the bandages, trying to locate the lips. Finally, he parted the bandages and peeled open the mouth. The tongue raised up and waggled, the wooden clamp clamped around the end of the tongue, clacked around its teeth. 'I can't remove the clamp without removing the tongue.'

The surgeon let go of the mouth and the bandages slowly closed over the lips. Inside the closed mouth, the tongue went clacking. It was as though a woodpecker had been trapped in a cave.

'This is the second man I have seen like this,' said the King's man. 'What is going on here?'

The surgeon wrung his wrists in his hands. 'I don't really know,' he said. 'But I bet it's the swineherd.'

The King's man made his way to a doorway, in a barn of many doorways. On his way, he saw a hunch back surrounded by surgeons.

The hunchback met the eyes of the King's man. It was as if, under the curve of his back, his head was coming out of a shell like a turtle. His back was covered in plum-looking boils.

The surgeons took their blacksmiths tools from the fire. When they fit them over the boils, they split and drained a grey liquid. The barn filled with the smell of sweet licorice.

The King's man is a short man. A man without fear. *I am to be hanged*, he thought.

He walked down the hill to the pigs.

Every board of every wall swelled outwards. Boards were broken and left walls full of gaps. When the King's man stepped close to a wall, the wall immediately jutted with snouts, pink, brown, black and white, snorting and grunting into the air.

Here was the swineherd, staring through a hole.

The swineherd heard the King's man and motioned him over.

The King's man obeyed and, coming, he too looked through a hole.

There was a pale yellow pig. It glowed in light from a crack in the roof.

'She trampled her own children,' said the swineherd. 'I won't describe it. They're scattered now in the dark.'

The pig stood so stiffly like its legs were wood dowels and it breathed as if its lungs were a bag full of rocks. As it stared back at the swineherd and the King's man, its mouth produced dollops of foam.

'I had planned to feed her to the King,' said the swineherd. 'And now the King's starving himself.'

'I am looking for the prince,' said the King's man.

The swineherd swallowed. 'I can't help you,' he said.

'Where is the prince?'

'He was taken.'

'Taken by who?'

'I don't know.'

The boards around them were snapped outward, some

of them inward. There were holes all through the wall. The pig must have been ramming its head through the walls. But there it stood motionless, breathing and attempting to growl. Its teeth had grown up through its snout and it could not fully open its mouth.

'The King always eats,' said the swineherd. 'He must always eat. He is in charge of the Body. What he does not eat, he gives to the criminals. This is the means by which the kingdom may function. The King must share with criminals his food.' He turned away from the pig and saw the small King's man. 'I cannot tell you anything which is not already obvious.'

The last light rolled away from the building and the pig drifted away into darkness. In a hole in the clouds, the King's man found the faint tracings of the moon, like an impression left in paper. The King's man thanked the swineherd and left, the pig's breathing faded and faded.

The King's man is a short man. He will be hanged.

He walked down the hill to the tavern. The tavern is dark and full of men with long beards and various appendages missing, eyepatches, empty pant-legs, hooks, black spaces where once there were teeth. They compared their knives, stabbing their huge shares of meat on the table.

The King's man orders a solitary beer and drinks alone in the dark.

Two impostors. One for the knights and one for the surgeons. Who are the impostors? Are entities of a foreign power? Or are they our own traitors? Further, why make the King's man go to all the effort of going farther and farther down the hill? Was everyone in concert?

The King's man thought nothing about this. He thought only, *I am to be hanged.*

He had walked around this world alone, and was determined to leave it alone, yet still the criminals drew his attention.

'King's man!' one said. He had two different colored eyes and an enormous black beard like a suspended explosion of soot. 'Will they really hang you tomorrow?'

The King's man nodded solemnly; his beer was amber colored.

'Too bad,' the bearded man said. 'We need more short men around.' He riled up the rest of them: one man with a bald head, one eye and sharpened teeth who had been deep in thought; a woman with no nose, no ears, and two beautiful eyes, sharp and dark, like a Sphinx; and one man with a red beard equally as bushy as the black beard, only this man had no teeth at all and a scar that ran around his face like the ring of a planet.

'Here's to the King's man, loyal and tiny,' said the black-bearded man. 'May we see him in Hell when he rests.'

They bash their stone mugs so beer scatters the table and soaks into their meat, which they share readily with the King's man. In places it is warm, in places it is cold. The King's man gnaws on a rib.

'We used to be knights,' said the blackbearded man. 'Believe it or not. Even her.' He pointed at the woman. 'We stayed for the King. We the Knights Order—'

They said in unison, '—serve only the King.'

The bone pile on the table was so immense it was as if they could reconstruct the full animal.

'That is,' continued the black-bearded man. 'Until we were dragged back into life by the surgeons.'

The four criminals all became downcast. Finally, the bald man spoke. 'I killed fifteen men for the King,' he said. 'Then I took an axe in the head.' He ran his finger quickly around the great scar running at an angle down his face. 'He hit me up top, then dragged in the blade all the way through the back just to finish the job. And now I'm alive.' He turned dour again and tore a strip of meat off a bone with his teeth.

The woman spoke with an accent. 'I poisoned ten women for the King. But the tenth did not fully die. She took revenge with a cleaver.' She traced her fingers from her ears to her nose.

The red-bearded man beside her put his hand over hers, almost like a brother. He began to open his mouth, but it appeared that it caused him great pain to speak. He made only clicks full of spit. He eventually held out his hands and uncurled his fingers. Both thumbs were missing. He nodded to the black-bearded man who uncurled nine of his own fingers.

'Seventeen?' said the King's man. 'You killed seventeen men?'

The red-bearded man nodded. Thankful, he withdrew his fingers.

'It is the prerogative of the King to keep knights alive,' said the black-bearded man. 'But it is the duty of the knight to die for his King. We believe we die gracefully, spilling out life on the battlefield, but then we wake up in the surgeon's tent, monsters, bandaged, useless to the king. It is too shameful. I cannot wield a sword.' With effort he tried to reach his own shoulder. His face contorted as if possessed by demons but made little progress toward his shoulder. The bald man reached it for him, pulling the black-bearded man's shirt down to reveal only scar tissue and what might have been a dislocation that had never properly healed.

'The King needs every man he can get,' said the bald man. 'But the Knights Order will not take us. Still, the King sends his compliments.' He gestured at the pile of bones and meat on the table.

'So, what is it you do now exactly?' said the King's man.

'We steal,' said the black-bearded man.

'And murder,' said the bald man.

The woman made a circle with two fingers then ran another finger in and out. The toothless man painfully nodded.

'And the King pays you in meat?'

'No,' said the black-bearded man. He took a rib and held it like an ear of corn to his lips. 'Our crime is inevitable. That cannot be stopped. And it is the same for our King.' He closed his eyes, as did the others. Then they all put their hands on their hearts. 'Our King cannot be stopped. We the Knights Order serve only the King.'

They opened their eyes and resumed eating the meat.

But the King's man continued. 'Stopped from what?'

'Whatever he starts.'

'What does he start?'

The black-bearded man paused. 'A King is compelled to do what he wants, to whomever he wants. If what he starts he can't finish, we finish. And then we call it a crime.'

'What is the King's crime?'

They were taken aback. 'A King does no crime.'

'Then what is your crime?'

'Our desire.'

They laughed and continued gnawing the bones, flesh spilling from their lips and the bone pile growing. They did not close their mouths and the splashing of meat sounded like pigs having sex. The King's man was going to be sick.

He emptied his stomach outside the tavern, then stared at the moon. It was huge now. Like some terrible face of some terrible god.

The King's man is a short man. But atop the gallows, he was the tallest man in town, aside from the executioner. Every shop and street was empty. They had left their homes to see the execution of the King's man.

The King sat in a throne arranged before the gallows, with the princess in his lap like a cat. She wore the special jewelry, the gold which once belonged to the prince.

The Knight of Reason stepped through the crowd and stood before the gallows. From the dirt, he looked up at the King's man on the high platform of the gallows. 'You are accused of high treason, not fulfilling your duties as to the protection of the progeny of the King. How do you plead?'

The King's man did not pay attention, only watched the princess and the King. The King was kissing her fingers.

'I plead as guilty as the King,' said the King's man.

There was quiet laughter of delight in the crowd. Even in his execution, the short man was cracking jokes. The King did not notice however, as he was busy now biting the fingers of the princess, popping them into his mouth, where they disappeared like olives.

'We have lost the prince,' he said. 'And look,' his hands bound, he gestured at the King and princess. 'We will lose the princess in a matter of days when our hungry King sneaks into her room and puts her piece by piece into his mouth. What the King himself cannot devour he will give to the criminals to suck clean at the bar.'

The King's man had never said such witty barbs. A man-eating King! A King with designs on his daughter! Truly reaching his highest point now, it was a pity to see the joke man go.

'I the King's man-' began the King's man.

They dropped the King's man through the floor. The rope caught tight and the King's man's little feet dangled fairly high above the ground.

It began slowly, the rain of applause. But as it grew louder, the princess cried out. The King had bitten a hole in her finger.

Death Comes to the old Lady, Paris - Roger Camp

Heartfelt Confusion: A Personal Puzzle
by Yuan Changming

More than once in the depth of
Darkness have I strongly felt
The whole earth shaking
But only to realise the next day

There was no earthquake at all

Perhaps, it's because my deformed heart
Beat hard like a seismic vibrations, or
Rather, I am the only one lying at night
Who happened to feel the quake?

Von Zimmer 2805
by Nicole Chvatal

After Unsolved Mysteries, "A Death in Oslo"

Grab as much as you can leave

No prints, black lace and a briefcase

Of live rounds

To disturb, dab *Ungaro*

From Italian blazer lapels

Cut out labels

Teeth imprinted in isotope

Acid to disappear

When French was preferred

Order in Flemish

From a small town in Belgium that won't forgive

Use a fountain pen to check in:

Jennifer Fairgate of Verlaine

Kroner thick folded in half

Leather trench hidden

Cash only.

The Case of the Radiator
by Bob Selcrosse

The great boy detective had eyes like a snake and skin like a worm. I approached him in an alley, under the lines and lines of washing.

He was staring up at an air-conditioning unit, which was barely holding on under the window.

'I don't trust machines,' he said.

'Nor do I,' I said.

'It's as if they could turn at any moment.'

'Yes, as if they all had minds of their own.'

'Yes, as if everything we did was to suit their minds and not our own.'

'As if we were only living to carry them on.'

We pondered a minute in silence. There, in the alleyway.

'I've been approached by a missing woman,' I said.

He looked at me funny and I patted his shoulder.

'Her sister is missing. They're twins, spitting images of each other. Only one is missing an-'

'An eye,' he said.

Cold shot up my spine.

'How did you know?' I said.

'She works at the pharmacy.'

I clicked my tongue. Of course he knew, he had his grandparents.

'She pays well,' I said.

He turned and looked at me. 'I'm on another case,' he said.

'Oh yeah?'

He nodded.

'Ok,' I said.

He watched the air conditioning unit for a moment. I noticed it had deposited a fair pool of fluid on the gravelly street beneath it. The fluid was rust colored and had a stale smell coming off it.

I removed the little divalproex sodium pill and held it in front of his nose.

He grabbed it. 'Whose is this?' he said.

'The pharmacist's.'

'What do you mean the pharmacist's?' He said it snappily. I got the sense he was spiraling into one of his moods.

'I mean her sister,' I said. 'She's on it.'

He held up his hand. 'Divalproex sodium.'

'Yes. Three-thousand milligrams a day.'

'That's extreme mania,' he said.

'I know,' I said.

He held the little pill in both hands and just stared at it.

'Why didn't you show me this sooner?'

'I mean, is 'missing woman' not enough?'

He squeezed the pill in his fingers. A number of lights went on in his head. He set off like a rabbit from the sound of a shot.

We came into a public area and did not run but walked as

quickly as we could.

I caught up with him. 'To the boardwalk?' I said.

'The boardwalk?' he said. 'No, no, no.' He walked with his whole body tense like a little boy soldier. 'Not the boardwalk.'

'The night market?'

He shook his head. 'No, no.'

We turned through a wet market full of tanks and ice chests and women smoking cigars and slipping out huge fish from hills of ice. They beat their cleavers so the fish heads flew off like bars of soap.

The great boy detective and I walked shoulder to shoulder and weaved in and out of the older people shuffling their feet and dragging their fingers through produce.

I caught my breath. 'But if she's off her pills. Even just for two or three days. Won't that swing her into withdrawal?'

'Maybe,' said the great boy detective.

'So maybe she'll go to the boardwalk and buy some.'

'I don't think so.'

We came to the section of fruit and dry goods. The great boy detective stopped in front of a fruit stand piled with jujubes, starfruit and cherries. The fruit seller sat reading a newspaper, with his feet on a box and his butt in a soft armless camping chair.

The great boy detective stopped and stared.

'What is it?' I said.

He walked to the man and snatched his newspaper. The man spilled out of his chair and lifted his hand to beat the boy, but then saw clearly who it was and stood patiently until the great boy detective might return it. 'Sorry, sir,' the man said. He had taken off his cap and held it in his hands.

We looked at the newspaper. On the final page: *One Night Only. Ride Dr. Z's Dirigible to the Forever World.* And in a little picture: a man with a bald head and an enormous black beard.

'Zelazny,' I said.

The great boy detective agreed.

We arrived at white-gabled house with two-stories.

The house had a lawn and a fence and a little wood gate.

The great boy detective knocked on the door and a voice yelled at us from inside to come in.

Here were two getting up in age, bundled in their armchairs and shivering.

The floor in front of them was stained with the heat and now the absence of a radiator.

'We're so happy you're here,' said the husband, his expression like a little happy lamb.

'We've been so cold,' said the wife. 'So c-cold.'

'Have you any notion as to where the radiator fled?' said the great boy detective.

'Not I,' said the husband.

'Not I,' said the wife.

The great boy detective tried every window and inspected every door. We conspired in the kitchen.

'Do you pity the old?' he said.

I must admit, I never think about the old. 'I do not,' I said.

'May I whisper you a secret?' he said.

I bent my ear. He stood up on his toes. 'I have two at

home,' he said.

He had told me this before. He seemed to find ways of telling me every few months. It seemed he needed to tell it to me. He had no one else to tell it to.

He walked through the kitchen, trailing his fingers on the counter tiles, from smooth to grout, smooth to grout, until he came to the cupboards.

'The funny thing,' he said. 'Contrary to our deepest fears, the old never leave their house.'

'Sure they do,' I said. 'How else would they escape?'

'They don't escape. They stay.'

The great boy detective held his finger before his lips and prepared his fingers on the final cupboard's handle. He indicated my gun. I prepared it at the cupboard. With supreme enunciation the great boy detective mouthed, *One. Two. Three,* then flung open the cupboard.

An enormous man leapt from the counter and onto the floor. Resembling a human hand, he spun around. He was like a frog made of white skin. His eyes were enormous. He was perhaps ninety years old. I trained my gun and we pursued him up the stairs.

However, upon reaching the second floor, the great boy detective did not immediately follow the breathing—which was obviously coming from the room at the end of the hall—but detoured to the bathroom.

'What are you doing?' I said, my gun still ready and aimed in the direction of the breathing. I leaned against the doorframe of the bathroom.

He was standing on a small stool to reach the medicine cabinet. 'Did you see that man's eyes?' he said.

'Not at that moment,' I said. I had been too afraid of his nakedness.

'If you do not keep your machines oiled,' he said. 'They break. We're at the brink of a destruction, I think, because of lack of concern for the aged.'

He rifled through the medicine cabinet. A number of the orange RX bottles fell into the sink.

Finally, he obtained a tiny white bottle with a teal nipple-lid, which he promptly unscrewed.

'Bimatoprost,' he said. He leaned his head back, pulled down his eyelid and shot drops from the bottle inside. Blinking, he squirt more drops in his hand and extended his hand toward me.

I smelled it. 'Smells like water,' I said.

'It is water,' he said. He handed me the little bottle. I glanced at the label. *Bimatoprost. Room temperature. Harry.*

'So what, it's solution?' I said.

He looked at me like I was a chimpanzee in a birdcage. 'You don't mix bimatoprost with water,' he said. 'You're saying someone's tampered with it.'

'Yes, but who—those two downstairs?' He pointed at the tight seem around the nozzle of the bottle. There was no sign of damage at all.

'Then, do you mean the pharmacist?'

He nodded patiently, or distractedly. 'That's exactly who I mean.'

He reached into the cabinet again and this time slid out a second identical bottle and shook it.

'Nearly empty,' he said. 'And look.'

I looked at the label. 'This expired today.'

'Yes.'

'I don't understand.'

'So the pharmacist sent the new dose a week early and those two bumblers downstairs cracked a new one open.'

'Nobody likes squeezing blood from a stone,' I said, shaking the near-empty bottle.

He shrugged. 'Nobody likes being cheated with water.'

He always got me. I was like a mosquito in his hands. I still held my gun, but it drooped. And in the silence, the backroom lungs swelled like a cave full of bats. Shuddering, I pretended I was only cracking my neck. 'So she planned this month's ago,' I said.

'I believe that's the case,' he said. He popped the near empty bottle in his pocket, then pointed at the one in my hands. 'You hold onto the fake one. We'll need it for evidence.'

He turned in the direction of the breathing, as if it had only just started. 'Well,' he said. 'No sense in delaying it any further.'

He shut the medicine cabinet and came out of the bathroom. We walked down the hallway. He put his hand on the door and looked at my gun. When he pushed it open, I held out my gun and stepped in first.

The man from the cabinet was now on the floor by the window. He held his legs to his chest and his chest swelled in and out. What light came through the window made the stray hairs of his skin glimmer like a spider's web after rain.

'I don't want to shoot you,' I said.

The man did not stir. He kept his eyes closed and his head down.

'Have you been in great pain?' said the great boy detective.

The man looked like an empty glove. He peeked out from under his hands. His eyes looked like unpolished brass.

'It's unfair, isn't it?'

The great boy detective came to kneel beside the man. He took the little bottle and unscrewed the teal lid, then gently pulled the man's eyelids up. They unfolded like flaps.

I kept my gun trained forward but, for the sake of the sake of the man's privacy, turned my head away.

The man tucked his eyes into his palms and his shoulders began to shudder.

We gave him a few moments, then led him back down the stairs.

The man came to his post in front of the recliners and the couple hungrily removed their slippers and socks.

'You found it!' said the husband.

'Thank god' said the wife. 'We won't freeze.'

The man arranged himself more perfectly on his knees and elbows, with his forehead resting on the backs of his thumbs.

The husband, shivering like a young animal, tried to scoot his easy chair closer to the radiator. The wife rested her heel on the old man's tailbone. As he inhaled, her foot tilted, and as he exhaled, it straightened.

'He's been in real pain,' said the great boy detective. He nodded to me and I produced the counterfeit bottle. 'Someone has tampered with your medications.'

I squeezed a little of the bottle's contents into my palm and let both wife and husband smell.

'I smell nothing,' he said.

'Smells like water,' she said.

'It is water,' said the great boy detective. He dropped the empty bottle in the husband's lap. 'Use this one instead. There's

The Case of the Radiator

a little bit left.'

I noticed a puddle of something collecting under the old man's face. It gathered on the floor between his elbows. A small pool of tears—the build up in his eyes had finally released.

When it became dark, we strolled through the neon night market and ate red bean waffles with tiny wooden forks. The night market sellers were a great deal more showy than those in your typical wet market. Vendors fired up their food stands under the night sky and called out to each other in couplets of poetry. *Ten dumplings a day! Keeps the doctor in pay!* Children walked around with shapes of the presidents' faces drawn in sugar and held on a stick. Street musicians were chased out but quietly snuck back in.

Under a quieter blue light, a stall of live fish. The great boy detective stopped at the tank of eels. He put his hands and face against the glass. The tank was big enough to fit him inside. But instead of him inside, it was a dozen writhing eels.

I poked at my waffle. True, it was our tradition to always celebrate after a case. But still, we had a missing woman on our hands. 'I don't understand,' I said. 'How is helping you with appliances, helping me with a woman?'

He did not turn away from the eels. He sighed, which fogged up the glass. Thus obscured, their eyes looked like black beads in a storm. 'What did we learn today about the radiator?' he said.

'The radiator has glaucoma,' I said.

'Is this common?' he said.

I shrugged. Nearby, an older bearded man handed out red miniature fishing nets to six girls surrounding a small tub of clownfish.

'Maybe,' I said. 'Isn't that what happens when you get old?'

He shook his head. 'Medications,' he said. 'Whether it is a radiator, planer, or sawhorse, there is proper care and improper care. Those two bimbos wouldn't know proper care if it burst their stomachs. That's why we have doctors and pharmacies.'

He turned away from the eels. 'I'm enjoying the market,' he said. He grabbed me by the sleeve and pulled me around like I was his brother. 'And how many days do we have?' he said.

'Two days now.'

We slipped through the dense crowd. The great boy detective suddenly stopped.

We stared at a balloon salesman.

In a sea of perhaps a thousand heads, there arose a large stack of balloons. They were so brightly colored it was as if they were not made of latex, but of shined porcelain. They were bigger than basketballs and there about thirty total, in pink, and green, and blue, and yellow, and purple. There were enough balloons perhaps to lift a small child into the sky.

'I want one,' said the great boy detective.

But we were frozen in a sea of eyes. The balloons drifted away from us.

I lifted the great boy detective onto my shoulders. Pursuing balloons, we bottlenecked in an alley. It was as if humankind would overwhelm the city and our bodies would burst through the walls.

By the time we had escaped the alley, the balloons had already vanished. We had come to the aqueduct, wide enough for only two passing gondoliers at a time. The balloon salesman must have crossed one of the footbridges and slipped into another alley.

I lowered the great boy detective to stand on his own. There was a kind older pinwheel salesman with his pinwheels arranged beside the canal. I motioned toward them, but the great boy detective's watch alarm beeped. 'How many days, one more time?' he said.

'Two,' I said.

'See you tomorrow,' he said.

He left through the alleys toward his grandparents' house.

Heading home, I caught sight of something like a small creature rolling around in the dark. When I touched it, it was only paper. I unfolded it. Surrounded by tigers and flames on the page, the Great Zelazny stared up at me.

sure
by Mark D Cart

it sounds
as if the rain

is coming up
for air again

me reduced
to name-calling

lacking all
else a noun

Not Waving if You Look Long Enough
by Alex Werner

The drowning woman waves her hands, fighting above the crest of incoming tide. When her head breaks the water, she sees a fluorescent green frisbee stuck in white sand. The discarded child's toy begs her to swim back to shore, pick it up, and create a moment of joy. It's the last thing she sees as hands pull her down.

I should have had more fun.

#

Just yards from the body washed up on the beach, Detective Smith notices a neon green frisbee stuck in the white sand.

She points at it, "Bag that."

Instead of doing as ordered, her partner-in-training, Detective Stevens, motions for a crime scene tech to bag the frisbee. Smith grits her teeth. He thinks his daddy dying a lieutenant means he doesn't have to earn his place, but he also works in a precinct where everyone knows his father named him Steven Stevens and called him Stevie. Maybe the two things cancel each other out, and he'll do some work.

"Couldn't this just be an accidental drowning?"

Stevie's an idiot, but it's her job to enlighten him. "See her ankle."

Smith watches the light come on behind his eyes.

"Finger marks."

"Right. Someone pulled her under," She gestures toward the girl's hands. "Now, look at her fingernails."

"Broken."

"Right. Look closer."

He squats beside the body. The girl's hands point forward as if she dived into the cold sand instead of the frigid water. The young woman's still-wet hair forms a starburst around her bluing face. A breeze from the water bites Smith's cheeks.

"There's still blood visible after she was in the water. So, we need to find someone who looks like he drowned a sixteen year old girl who scratched the shit out of him."

"Why do you assume it's a man?"

Smith takes a deep breath. "It could be a woman, but she's a young, female victim of violent death. Odds are good she was killed by a man."

"Her name's Alison."

"I know that."

He stands. "Why not call her by her name?"

Smith doubts he will understand why she doesn't call the corpse by the person's name, so she walks toward the water. Smith scans the area for clues. Takes a step. Scans again. Behind her, Stevie follows protocol and scans for anything she misses.

Smith decides to reward his good detective work by explaining why she didn't say the victim's name. "Do you know how many more female murder victims we see than male?"

When Stevie doesn't answer, Smith turns to face him. Legs akimbo. Hands framing her hips. Her dark suit coat flutters out behind her. She notices Stevie wears a wrinkled white button up, khakis, and sneakers with a pea coat. No tie. No suit jacket. His badge on a lanyard.

"To stay good at my job, I need to look at women's bodies without imagining they're me. I use their names to honor them to their loved ones, but they aren't their corpses. So, I don't call the body by their name."

"Seems relevant."

Fury edges against Smith's will to maintain control. "I've been on the police force as long as you've been alive. I have the highest solve rate in the district. I don't need you to verify my reasoning is relevant. You asked a question. I answered because you deserve the opportunity to learn. If you keep treating me like you're doing me the favor of accepting feedback, I will make sure you end up on narcotics stakeouts from here to eternity."

His cheeks redden. "I'm sorry."

Smith returns to searching out clues. Stevie follows. Something green catches Smith's eye. The winter sand has almost buried this discarded item, but she thinks it's another frisbee. If no one had come out to walk their dog this morning, would the sand have covered their victim too? Made her just another discarded thing.

After a few steps, Stevie says, "Wait."

Smith turns to him.

"I know you're a good detective. I know everyone says I got this job because my dad died a lieutenant."

She raises an eyebrow.

He holds his hands up in the universal sign of surrender. "And I know they're right. I should also know better than to act like I'm in charge."

He shoves his hands into his pockets and stares beyond her.

Smith offers an olive branch she's unsure he deserves. "It's not entirely your fault. Delegating instead of following orders and acting like people need your approval comes naturally when you're born with a penis. But recognizing shitty behavior isn't the same as fixing it."

She turns to resume her task, but Stevie walks away from the water.

Squinting into the sun's glare, he points. "There's a car in that lot."

She shields her eyes and spots the gray sedan. They walk toward the vehicle, and further from the crashing waves, Smith hears a car alarm. The empty stretch of beach is only accessible by the surrounding homes and a small hotel attached to this parking lot.

As they reach the spot where the concrete's edge blurs into the fluttering blanket of sand, Smith holds out an arm, staying her partner. She looks for footprints, dropped items, anything. She's not hopeful there's much to find, but she doesn't want to walk over a clue. Satisfied there's nothing to disturb, Smith waves Stevie toward the car. She spots another frisbee irreverently tossed into the sparse grass on the far side of the building.

The car's alarm is louder. It's warning them that the trunk is popped up. The alarm distorts and elongates as the battery dies.

"Remind me to ask the techs how long a battery lasts. If this is our vic's car, she might not have been in the water long."

"If she drowned last night, the tide would have taken her out. It turned inland this morning," Stevie says staring into the car's back seat.

Smith, who's examining the exterior of the vehicle, says, "I'm not much for memorizing tide charts. Good you knew that."

"I sail."

This one line from Stevie leaves Smith grimacing and rolling her eyes toward heaven. It's not a crime to be an irritating parody of white male privilege, she reminds herself, continuing around the car.

Apart from the key stuck in the ignition, the sedan is

empty. She's never known a teenage girl with a car this clean. Her own vehicle is always spotless. No good can be found comparing herself to the corpse, so Smith, Stevie in tow, walks down the driver's side toward the trunk.

A woman exits the back door of the hotel. "It's about time you got here. I called about that car almost an hour ago."

Smith walks over to the woman, taking in defining features. A streak of gray through straight brown hair. Green eyes. Small birthmark at her throat. Tattoo of an anchor on the inside of her ankle.

"I'm Detective Smith," she says showing her badge, "I'm not here in response to your call, but I'll try to help."

Smith extends her hand and the woman shakes it. "I'm Alison. The breakfast half of the bed and breakfast."

What are the odds this woman and the victim would share a name? Smith doesn't see it, but she senses Stevie smirking. Smith almost bumps into her partner as she turns. She motions him back toward the car and asks the witness, "Can you give me one second?"

Walking over to Stevie, Smith instructs, "Get the techs up here. Call dispatch. Find out why no one's responded. Do a circuit of the building. If you find something, radio me, but give me a chance to step away from her before you say anything."

Her partner nods and walks around the side of the hotel. Feeling petty, Smith hopes he's annoyed to be left out of questioning the witness.

She walks back to Alison and sees another castoff green frisbee on the hotel's patio. "Can you tell me why you called the police?"

"I thought it was weird there was a car back here." Like many witnesses Smith speaks to, she seems nervous. Glancing behind her. Folding her arms. "We only have one guest. It's the off season, so the employees park up front. I saw a guy back here, and I thought he was sneaking onto the beach. I don't usually call people in, but something seemed wrong."

"Can you be more specific about what seemed wrong?"

Alison pauses before saying, "He started the car and pushed buttons. Opened the gas tank, turned on the wipers. He stopped when the trunk popped. I thought he should know how to open his own trunk." Her eyes widen as if remembering, and she continues, "The 911 operator told me not to close it. Is that okay?"

"Absolutely, Alison. I wish half the people I talked to were half as helpful as you. Can you tell me anything else? Anything about the man? Height, weight, clothes?"

"It was dark, but he walked all hunched up. I thought he might be wet."

A beep over the radio interrupts Alison's story, and Stevie says, "Smith. I need backup. Now."

There's a vibrato of fear beneath the demand, and Smith chooses to ignore his failure to give her time to step away from the witness.

"Go back inside and lock the door. Make sure no one enters or leaves the building until an officer says it's safe."

Pushing the radio's talk button, "What's happening?"

"I found an officer injured in the alley. I have dispatch on my cell."

Smith runs to the alley, a poorly lit gap between the hotel and a plank privacy fence that obscures the house next door. She keeps a hand on her gun until she spots her partner kneeling on the ground next to a young, male officer. He's no more than a child. Neither of them is more than a child compared to Smith.

She looks at the officer, "What happened?"

"Dunno, ma'am. I came in response to the 911 call about

the car. I saw this soaking wet guy, so I stopped to talk to him. He takes off. I followed him down here. He stabbed me."

He seems to lose his train of thought. His eyes don't focus, "I just ran after him. Left my radio and my phone in the car. It was stupid."

"Why did you come alone?"

"We're short this week."

Stevie interrupts, "He's lucky it's cold."

For the first time, Smith notices his teeth are chattering. Her partner has taken off his shirt and wears just his pea coat. His hands move expertly, tying strips of the shirt around the officer's abdomen to keep pressure on the wound.

"Cold slows blood flow."

Smith feels a stir of pride. Stevens might not be hopeless. "He's lucky you found him. My first aid skills leave something to be desired." Patting him on the shoulder, Smith says, "Nice work."

A car drives past, illuminating a splash of green at the end of the alley. Smith walks that way, taking in her surroundings as she thinks through what must have happened. The man brought the officer down the alley to get out of sight. After the man stabbed the officer, he would have come back this way not onto the beach where he'd be exposed. At the end of the alley, Smith walks a few paces down the road to the left and sees only a row of houses. Moving back to the right, Smith sees the officer's police car two blocks down.

She returns to the sidewalk in front of the alley and glances to the dumpster where the flash of neon green she spotted earlier reveals itself to be another frisbee. On the ground a few feet up the sidewalk, there's a small metal box. She pulls on a latex glove and kneels to pick it up. It's one of the magnetic hide-a-keys people put under their cars. She shakes it, hears nothing, and wonders if it held the key now stuck in the car's ignition.

Some indistinct noise or movement to her right clangs an internal warning bell in Smith's head. She stands up. There's a man inches from her, holding a knife.

"Give me that." He slurs around the bloodied gash of his mouth, gesturing at the box.

Smith tosses it toward him. The man leans over to grab the hide-a-key, and she draws her gun, aiming at his center as he stands. "One step, and I pull the trigger."

He stops. "You a cop?"

"Detective. Put your hands in the air. You can drop the knife and that box too."

"Fuck." The man says, the hide-a-key and knife falling from his raising hands.

He's closer now, and Smith sees his face is covered in claw marks. Eyes swollen. The salt water must have stung. That girl fought so hard. She should still be alive.

The corner of the building blocks her from seeing down the alley, so keeping her eyes and the gun trained on the suspect in front of her, Smith pushes her radio's talk button. "Stevens, I need backup."

"Smith, I'm…"

She cuts him off. "Now, Stevens."

She waits for what must be thirty seconds. Her hand twitches. She pushes the button again, "Stevens. Backup. Now."

He doesn't respond

Smith glances around the suspect, trying to see down the alley. The man moves toward her. "Don't move," she says returning her attention to him.

The man stays still, but he's slightly closer.

Smith pushes the button again, "Stevens. This is serious. I

need help."

A few seconds later, he responds, "Can you hold on a second? I'm a little busy."

Seizing the opportunity of her distraction, the suspect lunges toward her. Without a thought, Smith pulls the trigger.

Her partner runs around the corner from the alley, shouting, "I'm sorry. I didn't want to leave Officer…"

Smith waves away Stevie's excuses, dropping to the ground beside the suspect. She tries to apply pressure to his chest. As her hands coat with this man's pooling blood, she has little hope she can help him.

Protocol says you call your partner to do the handcuffing. Following protocol with a partner like hers is about as useful as having an extra arm in the middle of your ass. Smith thinks of what happens to her career now. Desk duty. Paper work. Therapy.

"Just let me explain." Stevie continues talking like he thinks words make this right.

Pressing her hands to the chest wound, Smith stares at the frisbee on the dumpster lid.

"I didn't mean for this to happen."

She almost can't believe Stevie's capacity to imagine his words matter when things have gone so wrong because of his actions. Smith's rage boils. She breathes in, trying to calm herself. The scents of gun smoke and blood and the salt of ocean spray fill her nostrils. She's the one who follows protocol, but it's Stevie who comes out of this smelling like roses.

"At least he didn't get away."

Pressing bloodied palms to the ground, Smith rises to her feet and grabs her partner's jaw in one bloody hand. It takes everything in her not to claw at his face and make him look as broken as the man on the ground. As her nails dig into his jaw, she uses her other hand to press the top of his head.

"Please, listen to me." Her partner continues to talk around Smith's attempts to physically shut his mouth.

Smith releases his face and pushes him hard with both hands against his chest emphasizing her words, "Shut. The. Fuck. Up." She steps back from him, panting, "I've heard enough excuses. I asked you for help what three or four times? I could have died. Instead, I had to shoot a man. I hope like hell he deserved it, but your words don't fix this. So, stop talking."

Seeing he's shivering in his pea coat, Smith softens fractionally, but she hisses through her teeth, "You needed to stay with the other officer, so get back there."

Stevie looks like he wants to say more, but he walks back down the alley.

Returning to the dying man, Smith watches his body go still and his eyes turn to glass. A neon green glint bounces off their surface. Smith looks behind her at the frisbee. She leaves the dead man to his after-life.

She watches the frisbee almost convinced there's only one, and it's following her. A crime scene tech appears, placing bags over her hands to protect the evidence. An officer leads her to a patrol car, and sitting in the back, she glances out the rear window. A female crime scene tech fusses over Stevie. He laughs.

The detective feels certain her partner will get a promotion for saving that officer while she sits behind her desk. She faces forward with her hands at rest in her lap. Her body is evidence now.

The officer gets behind the wheel. They drive toward the fluorescent green frisbee. It feels like that discarded child's toy begs her to pick it up. Throw it. Create a moment of joy.

I should have more fun.

Murder at Murphy Manor
by Timothy Arliss OBrien

A party, late eve, a brief get together
One night at Murphy Manor.
Too many had arrived, and not enough left by the end of the night.

I wanted to enjoy my evening,
But I've been out of my mind,
Skyscrapers are growing through my head.
Angels are trespassing,
And devils have an invite,
Plus one.

The only question is,
Who killed the professor,
Also, the composer's been found dead too
Luckily I, the poet,
Am alive to tell the tale.
The opera is only in act 3,
And who knows who else might be found dead,
By curtain.

And ere we have a mystery,
Who was the culprit,
And what was the murder weapon?
For each demon had an invite,
And everyone had a plus one.

Yet now that I am off the streets,
My poetic imagery dissipates.

****

Onward ye sloth like selfless soul,
For we a poem have to write.

A mystery needs solved
And my there's so many in question,

But where oh heavens do we start.

During the murders at hand it seems as all parties were ceremoniously preoccupied.
Gluttony occupied himself in the kitchen while Envy looked on in jealousy,
Sloth took a nap in the upstairs bedroom while Lust hosted a variety of lovers on a pillow nearby.
And Greed went through everyone's coat pockets while Pride fixed her outfit in the mirror every few minutes.

Asmodeus swears he was with Persephone and Beelzebub in the basement, surely getting high and plotting violence.
And Lucifer, Baphomet, and Lilith were in the attic tripping far out on acid.

I personally think that Shiva, Euronymous, and Dracula had most to do with the aforementioned crimes, but tracking them down is a feat impossible.

****

The night grows late and the shadows deepingly menacing,
And the threat of more murder hides and heckles around each corner.

Oh no! I've found my fate to late,

For I am next to die.

With knife in hand I at last learn,

That I alone was murderer

This whole time long.

Who Killed the Middle Class?
by L. Fid

"The cold rain began, a slanted pelting of big drops. Beneath the streetlight's orange dome, the gutters already ran black. Somewhere, a dog barked."

Hey, that's no dog!

The solid, middle-aged woman pushed the typewriter's carriage release back and to the left, then leaned down and cocked her head out the window.

"Hey, Fran! Stop barking, wouldja? Tryin' to work here!"

"Aw, gitover y'self already! PFFFFT!"

There were a few more hoots and catcalls up and down the fire escape before the fuzzy sound of sleet hitting brick, glass, and metal swallowed the squawking whole. The ashtray spattered on the sill: ping, ping, ping. She pulled it out, briefly scanning the desk before jamming it into a stack of papers.

She turned back to the wet opening, yanked out a wood rod. The window, taped over since an irate client blew up last summer, slammed into slush, splashed her wool overcoat.

She lay her stubby, nicotine-stained fingers back to the keys, read over the line, thinking, where was I going with this?

At least the barking stopped.

A soft rapping, almost a feline scratching, on the front door's frosted glass pane diverted her literary aspirations. A silhouette appeared, disappeared, reappeared according to the whims of the hall light.

Damn it! She hated meeting people like this. Her office manager -- her sole, part-time employee -- she should be getting the door! But, the irate client again... Pel would be out for a while, recovering from wounds.

Still, why does Pel get to stay home?!

Here I am, with worse! Many times over. Working!

Rap. Rap. Rap.

She ignored the pleas from the outer office, turning to look into a slice of silt-smeared window sky. Truth is, she missed Pel in many ways, not least because Pel knew how to engage the yokels early on -- set the tone of professionalism and conspiratorialism just right. The B.S. people want, what they had come to believe existed, from a P-I Agency in a "picturesque" neighborhood.

On her own, she thought she came off as a buffoon, especially if she tried to play those people-person games. In a self-defeating defense, she mostly played the role of a time-constrained hard ass. Hard to do when you're answering your own door in a dark, empty office. Shit. The scratchy rappings were now accompanied by "yoo hoo"s, whispered periodically.

She had not yet moved from behind the desk. Maybe they'd move on. Maybe it was the window slam sound. Or another bill collector. Better stay quiet.

"Helloo! M. Nutter. We'd like to hire you. Yoo hoo. Yoo hoo."

She waded through a greasy tide of fast-food wrappers ebbing around the back of her desk, strode the ten feet from back office to front, unlocked the door, yanked it open.

"Can you read?" She asked.

"Why, of course. 'M. Nutter, Private Investigations, LTD,' it says right..."

"And what about here?" She pointed to the outer doorknob, noticed it was bare.

"GODDAMN YOU!" She shouted towards the stairs

at the end of the hall. "Stole it, again, those brats. Says, 'Do Not Disturb.' I'M A'GONNA FUCK YOU UP, DIRTBALLS, JIZZMOUTHS, WHEN I GET HOLDA YOU!"

She looked over the mark. Tall, thin, well-dressed, gender-neutral.

"Oh, come in, then. Come on."

They wore a raspberry beret, the kind you find at a second-hand store.

"Call me Nutter."

- - -

They explained their deal, methodically, in their-oh-so-way: a somnambulistic, metered droning, like a dead-voiced poet she'd watched one time down at the bookstore -- back in normal days.

Nutter started off feeling confused, then mild contempt -- a fear response for what she did not know. These kids, for one thing. First, they were all reclusive-suicidal emos, soulmate-searching stalkers. Now this, a dollop of pronoun sensitivities as cherry on top.

Still, it was far better than the other kinds of youth, or the sad-eyed man-boys, who kept cropping up in her peripheral zones; sometimes, her combat zones. Those bastards, fuck-heads, the right-wing shadow opposites, the haters -- she hated them, the haters, worst of all, of course.

Looking up and down the would-be client, she thought, we have this in common: those Proud Percenters and Prayer Boys, whateverthefuck they called themselves now... They hate me, with my butch-as-fuck in-your-faceism, as much as they do you twee they-thems. So, we'll be on the same side in the Fight.

They used the initial J as their name. J offered a surprisingly convincing case for the outlandish claim. Studiously ignoring the seductive patter, Nutter felt a determination set into her head like concrete. No matter the morality, or any audacious fuckyou-edness in the cause -- nor even the unlikely possibility of a rent-making payday -- she was not going to get drawn into this type of madness.

She was going to talk J off that ledge. Or, since fanaticism might be in play and the ledge their preferred position, she might just well just focus on getting them out and getting on with her night.

Ah, crap. She always was a sucker for political-economic debate.

She interrupted: "So, sure. More than anybody, it was Reagan that killed the middle class. I get it, I think. You're going with a, uh, show trial -- like Bertrand Russell with the American War on Vietnam tribunal in Switzerland, or whatever."

J started to respond, but Nutter raised her fist. She lifted three fingers. "Three things." She parked her butt on the edge of Pel's reception desk and prepared her dialectic.

"First, why Reagan? The dull edge of the sword, I'd say.

"What about the Powell Memo in '71, or the 'Crisis of Democracy' report in '75? That's when the ruling class realized the middle-class experiment was a bad idea, I'd say. Overeducated kids fuckin' around with the apple cart.

"So, they end free college, squeeze the COLAs, turn up the tax revolt.

"After that, that's when they hire the hit man, Reagan. Together they bust the unions, make deals with rednecks, fire up the neo-Nazis. The reason, the first cause, hidden behind dog whistles, fundamentalism, nationalism -- that never changes. It's simple.

"Make the rich richer.

"Trickle down, that's bullshit! Funnel wealth upward with tax cuts and corrupt privatizations. That's what it's all about.

"Bada-bing, bada-boom. Several bubbles later, we get the

foul fruit from the earlier seed, played as farce." Nutter made a hand flourish as if introducing a lounge act. "Trump and the Magats."

"But, just after... After the Gripfter... There was Clinton."

"Sure, Reagan tapped the middle class good, right in the forehead, and down it went. Then they got Clinton to finish the job.

"He's running, and lying, like they all do. Just after the Flowers leaks, he turns all warm and fuzzy to Nafta. And, whadayaknow, POOF. All his problems go away. Perot you-peopled, Bush senior vomiting on cable. Clinton, the best positioned, gets the assignment.

"It's him that delivers the final taps, the coup de grace. Not just Nafta, but more dismantled safety net, deregulated finance, a P.R.-manufactured air campaign to save Nato and the DoD for future forever wars, even without commies.

"Bush junior and Obama, of course, they dance on the decomposing body of the middle class. Same agenda, plus, direct cash infusions for billionaires. Patching holes in the bubbles. All this, so, finally, Trump can play Fuhrer at the gates of hell, and, now, peak Weimar, Biden can bring us back for a hot second to the normalcy of late-stage frog boiling.

"With all that, and more, why pick on the first hired hitman: brain-damaged Reagan? How 'bout the follow-on Bushes, Clintons, and such?"

J shifted their feet, attempting to occupy the brief pause. Nutter resumed with only a rhetorically dramatic missed beat.

"Especially, though, why not the billionaires?

"They took the Powell Memo to heart and built up the right-wing echo chambers, a giant murder machine that kills the middle class then, now, and forever -- while mock-worshiping a mythologized version of it.

"Those fucks, the billionaires and their senior VPs for

mass murder, they employ both: Republican deplorables and Democrat neoliberals. The whole narrow spectrum.

"So. That's number one. Reagan is just a stand-in for all the other murderers and, more importantly, their employers -- the donors and owners."

J opened their mouth. Nutter threw two fingers up, towards the unlit, but still visibly water-stained ceiling tiles.

"Second thing."

J leaned against a large plastic umbrella they'd brought, cocked their head to listen, conveying some attitude. Nutter settled more firmly onto the front of Pel's desk, still holding up two fingers.

"Numero duo. What are we doing? Setting up the middle class as some sort of innocent victim or idyllic goal state? The managers of empire get an ecologically damaging lifestyle, too? Erase the red lines, allow a few token changes, then it's okay?

"No way. It won't work.

"The social contract is gone. The only reason we ever got thrown such bones was to prevent socialist revolution, starting back in the thirties. Then, for anti-commie propaganda until the seventies.

"Unless we make that threat real again, suburbs are for landed gentry.

"You and me -- well, me anyway -- priced out, unless we time it right and ride a bubble inside.

"Who killed the middle class? Well, I would if I could.

"I'd kill the unreal idea of it, where working class people transform their mental identity into something they aren't, via debt and denial. And... unto misery, mostly, I tell you what, from what I've seen. It's them that drank the shitty Kool-Aid.

"And when things go rotten, this pretend middle is directed against the supposed lower, with fear and hate. Then off we go to the brownshirts. Somehow, these fools will even back a reality-tv huckster, their beloved hater-in-chief, to play out their zombie revenge fantasies.

"Fuck the middle class! Even though it's dead, it's still blocking the way to, well... any real reform, much less revolution."

Behind J, a shadow flitted across the translucent, wired glass embedded in the front door. Nutter swiped them to the side, pulled open the door, barged into the hall.

The lights flickered up and down in both directions, so it was hard to make out anything.

The door to the stairwell, next to the inoperative elevator, was just starting to close.

Nutter turned to run and everything went cockeyed.

- - -

"Whoa, there. Slow, slow." J had Nutter's elbow. They seemed to be working hard at keeping both their balances. "A doorknob sign, unworth the scene, to my mind, anyway. Come, come. Please continue."

J's words seemed far away as they steered them back inside from the spasmodically tilting hallway. Nutter staggered around Pel's desk and collapsed into a dangerously mis-wheeled wooden semicircle of an old office chair.

"What's wrong with me?" Nutter thought, spinning two feet into a filing cabinet before remembering. The sativa elixir concentrate -- to help with the writing. Pel's recommendation. The glass jar sat there on the desk, half empty, next to the delivery box adorned with a happy-face postit note, green.

That must be it. Or...

"Or," J continued, patiently, "I can pick up from where I was? Answer your concerns? Even though you seemed but halfway through your screed.... Are you sure you're not a he/him? You mansplain like a motherfucker."

Nutter felt strongly, proudly, that her gender had room for the likes of her -- despite periodic pronoun shifts among her longtime friends. She grimaced, kicked her feet and sent the chair towards a floor fan by the other wall. Through a tight smile and spinning arc, she said, "I do have one more thing." She raised a fist, unclenched it into the bird.

J tilted the umbrella sideways, threw their head back and laughed.

"Nutter, Nutter," they uttered as she crashed into the fan. "You seem unwell. Do you mind?" They leaned over the desk, picked up the jar. "Hmmm... This sort of thing, normally, a measuring device is used. But, I suppose, you... You just swig."

Still suffering from vertigo, Nutter nodded and leaned against the fan's dusty grill while J began a well-considered rebuttal.

Reagan's the man to pin the wrap on, for sure, J argued. That seventies stuff may have been necessary prelude. But the big turn, the swerve back for all of human history, away from rationalism and science and progress, to.... irrational exuberance, family values, and nasty little forever wars.

That was Reagan and Thatcher, the destructive duo of the eighties. Goodbye detente, goodbye grand bargains, goodbye middle class.

J was adopting some of Nutter's rhetorical flourishes -- good for them, she thought.

Besides, they continued, it's got to be him. All the true believers, a significant portion of the surviving bourgeoisie, still burn hard for the ole Gipper. They see him with Rambo biceps and an M60 -- the prototype for the same Drumpf delusion -- instead of the chickenhawk fakers and traitors they both really are.

Reagan was a brain damaged puppet, sure, J agreed, but a

powerful symbol still. So, who else to pin it on? Nobody. Ronny Raygun is The Killer, dead to rights.

Nutter watched the desk spill into itself. A stack of folders three feet high collapsed from one side to the other, setting off another pile. The event knocked the box and jar, Pel's gift, to the floor. "Oh, dear. I hope I was not the catalyst of this destruction to your, hm, organizational system." They started fussing around the desk, attempting to corral paper, making matters worse. Peripheral desk items, pens, paper clip holders, spilled over the edges.

Still floor fan-adjacent, Nutter observed from semi-recline, focusing on the jar as it rolled across the floor. It came to a stop beneath the desk's Formica fronting.

Wait a minute, she thought.

I didn't open that box. I didn't drink any weed concentrate. I don't remember any of that. Sure, I've been sipping cheap scotch since late morning, along with the antidepressants, supplements and cold meds, caffeine, nicotine. The usual.

But, then, why did I think I did?

Pretending to tidy up the desk, J turned to the question of the middle class as murder victim and started working up an argument. Right, thought Nutter, ready to direct her attention back into the stream of debate -- deal with that can of worms.

She leaned her cropped, scarred head back against the fan and tried to follow J into a complicated neo-Marxist, situationist worldview, by which groups of people reify into class identities. Their solution was to shake up the system with an unambiguous event, one that sears an image into the collective psyche for generations. The rightwing godhead consuming its own followers -- mass murdering us all. Ploughing the field for the seeds of revolution to come.

"Okay," Nutter said with a thick tongue, "I guess. You're sold on the idea, anyway. But, why me? Bodyguard? Investigator? A witness at your, hopefully viral, show trial, or, big event?

Hate to bring up money to a fellow traveler and all, but, this is an office, you know. I have bills."

There were shadows in the hall again. J was fiddling with their phone. Nutter flashed on a disconnected memory: a black-block anarchist handing J an aerosolizer in the hall, J spraying her in the face, Nutter staggering back, away from the delinquent chase and into the fog.

"Ah, Nutter," J looked up from the phone. "Don't sell yourself short. You're key to the festivities."

Nutter's mind's eye rose out of her body, out the window, past Fran and the other tenants who were at their windows, checking on the dwindling precipitation. Nutter floated over the city, above the low clouds. A ring of suburban hills resolved from soggy mist, bathed in resplendent sunlight. A giant robot Reagan with laser eyes and an energy whip wrought havoc -- kicking minivans across the park, eating t-ball players by the handful, slashing McMansions open like rotten fruit. She thought it might be taken down like an Imperial Walker, with a leg trap.

"Nutter, stay with me." The shadows in the hall emerged in stark outline. Three beefy men, clad in Proud Boy polo shirts, entered and surrounded J. "Don't worry. They're not what they seem." They set the phone against their leg.

"But you are, or you will be." J Leaned in, head tilted against the angle of the umbrella. "Fanatic, lone wolf, martyr... Fall, hm, gal?"

All four of them were crammed into the small front part of the office, Nutter still pressed up against the floor fan. She blinked in confusion as the jar seemed to roll away slightly from the desk, before she spied the black-whiskered, pink snout of Stealer, the office ferret.

"Devil's Breath got your tongue?" J did not notice Stealer, but made as if to spray an invisible mister. "Hm... Never mind." They pulled up the phone again and started twiddling. "We have what we need. A little deep fakery and your final manifesto will be ready to post. A psychedelic cog in my catastrophic plan." Using skin-tight, red leather gloves, they pulled a small electronic pin out of their beret, and lay the camera back in its case.

"The denouement, on video as well, has you being pummeled out there beneath that streetlight, and the surveillance camera above. The antagonists -- our fine, muscled friends here."

They arched a carefully drawn brow towards Nutter. Nutter was thinking about Stealer. He'd gone home with Pel, hadn't he? And, now, it seemed she did remember drinking the marijuana concentrate, with Pel. When was that? She wasn't thinking straight -- the Devil's Breath, or Burundanga, Scopolamine. She and Pel had used some once. The trip wasn't too bad, but the after effects... Jesus. She knew that the drug's uses were mostly violently criminal now -- what with the suggestibility and memory loss.

"Still nothing?" J cocked their head. "A bit disappointing. Anyway, show time." J motioned to the fake Proud Boys. It took all three to maneuver her into the hall.

J stayed behind and made their way to the back office. They read the few lines Nutter had managed to hack onto the page from the archaic typewriter. They pulled a phone from a plastic bag, propped it against the damp ashtray, and framed a tight video shot through the window -- one of a few backups in place. After some musing, they typed a few more letters onto the page and looked outside.

The boys still weren't in position. What was going on?

Pel and Nutter burst into the office.

Pel, wounds apparently healed enough to Capoeira their asses, had gone through the P.B.'s, or whatever they were, like butter. A few elegant kicks and elbows had left them hanging 20 feet over nothing in the elevator shaft. Nutter, rescued and vengeful, was still too drugged to do more than glare fiercely, swaying.

With practiced hands, J attached a sturdy climbing clip to the wall radiator, opened the window and backed out, arms controlling a coiled rope fore and aft. They'd finished their descent before Pel reached the window.

Stealer jumped up to the sill and hissed, then hopped back onto the desk near J's phone, which was still recording on full zoom. Two figures fought their way across the screen, Fran on all fours barking and chasing a theatrically overdone, zombie Reagan.

Nutter turned the typewriter's roller knob and read the new line: "The black water turned red."

She looked through the dark window at Fran splashing along the sidewalk after zombie Reagan. "We need to go after them," she said. "They're onto something."

Pel turned from the window's odd tableau to focus on Nutter. "You're high."

Stealer sat on his back legs and dooked.

Whistling in the Dark
by Nicholas Yandell

How do we not find it exhausting,
        Living lives,
                Born into mystery?

    We're thrown into this world,
        Helplessly absorbing,
           Ideas from other minds,
                Crawling our way,
                    Towards an impossibly
                            distant
                                light.
            We play detective,
                  Find those elusive clues,
Gather acres of evidence,
        Wondering all the while,
            Whether our investigative skills,
Are really effective enough,
        To find surety,
                    In our realities.

Knowledge is power,

        But also has limits.

                Will striving too far,
            Leave us untethered,
        Freewheeling,
    The outer reaches,
Of our minds?

           Are perceptions,
        Just malleable materials,
        Manageable enough,
        To keep our heads,
        From exploding,

                               With the volatility,
         Of all our surfacing quandaries?

Should we in necessity,
To ease our anxieties,
Just make peace,
With our unknowns?

                 Walking onward,

        Blind to the glaring expectations,

           Softly whistling in the dark.

The Art of the Never-Ending Ego
by Kate Falvey

You could, if you were so minded,
dab another descriptor onto the page,
something sunny like dazzle or
a blotch of razory silver,
glinting in a naughty knot of cursive,
a wink or arched curve of pencil
under a dramatic swath of glistening fringe.
The eye would be brimful and green,
the hair blue black and plummeting
into an iconic wave, slender with
edges, the dawn coming on, the night
relinquishing stars.

Whole pantries of noontide spill into kettles
and tins, the cakes are iced with vestiges of
sparkling and scintillating high notes, the brandy
will have to wait but its memory is wafting over the tart.
Crumbs are swept briskly into a stolid palm as
the afternoon wanes and sherries are brought devoutly forth.

She did it.
It was her all along.
It could have been no one else.
Had there been less blood,
one might have considered that dodgy
bloke with the plummy afterglow
and the nervy howitzer eyes.

One Thing I Won't Forget
by Karla Linn Merrifield

I learned Saturday I am only so much recycled star stuff.
Atoms of my body, albeit an original mix of matter,
date to one of the many Big Bangs of the multiverse.
I've been feeling old lately, but, really people, that old?
So said the astrophysicist on the auditorium stage
at the Zen Center symposium, an April afternoon's
inquiry into—Shhh! —nature and consciousness,
a search for the adjacent possible, whatever that is,
glimpses at answers to the many Big Issues of life.
In a room crowded, warm, Big Buddha Boy, I swooned!

Can you blame me, buddy, if two days later I pick
at the cuticle next to my lauded opposable right thumb,
looking for wisdom in dry skin, biting it off, spitting?
To think, pal, I've been alive since the beginning;
and I'll never die, even when our sun at last explodes.
I scratch my scalp; dandruff flakes off like memories
of childhood, adolescence, yesterday, and the day before that.
In a blink of cosmic time, I am of an age of agelessness: now.
I make a covenant with mystery employing every ancient
recombinant molecule of my mind, remark wonders never
cease.

A Glimmer of Intuition
by Jen Mierisch

FADE IN:

INT. COUNTY HEALTH DEPARTMENT OFFICE - DAY

In a cubicle, BETH FISHER (late 20s), sits staring at a computer screen, chin resting on her hand.

>   RICK (O.S.)
>   (from the next cubicle)
>   You catch Law & Order last night?

>   BETH
>   No, it's on my DVR. I was out last night.

RICK MYERS (late 20s), pops his head over the wall between his cubicle and Beth's.

>   RICK
>   You were out?

>   BETH
>   (startled)
>   Jesus, Rick, you're like a demented gopher.

>   RICK
>   Hot date?

>   BETH
>   Lukewarm date.

>   RICK
>   So ditch him and watch it with me. It was a great episode.
>   Stabler meets this guy who has a -

>   BETH
>   No spoilers, Rick!

DOLORES WARD (early 50s) walks into Beth's cubicle. Rick's head vanishes. Beth sits up straight and turns to face her.

DOLORES
Just spoke with Dr. Greene at County General.

BETH
More lung infections?

DOLORES
Eight this week, six retirees and two kids. Same pattern, acute symptoms, quick recovery. Several cases have occurred in the Long Pines retirement community.

BETH
Guess I'm going on assignment.

DOLORES
Three households agreed to be interviewed. I'll send you the names and addresses.

Dolores walks back down the hall to her office.

Rick walks to Beth's nameplate on the wall of the cubicle. He pretends to write on the nameplate with a marker.

BETH
What are you doing?

RICK
Just changing your name to Lieutenant Olivia Benson.

Beth tosses a package of tissues, hitting Rick, who laughs.

BETH
Be serious, Rick. As much as you'd love it, we work for the health department, not the NYPD.

RICK
(imitating the iconic Law & Order sound effect)
Dun-dunnn.

Beth rolls her eyes.

EXT. LONG PINES RETIREMENT COMMUNITY - DAY

A car, whose door reads "County Health Department" on the side, turns off the main road, driving past a sign that reads "Long Pines Retirement Community".

The car pulls to a stop in front of a neatly landscaped house. Beth exits the vehicle.

INT. ELAINE MCAULEY's HOUSE/LIVING ROOM - DAY

Beth stands with primly dressed ELAINE MCAULEY (late 60s) in Elaine's tidy living room.

BETH
Please don't go to any trouble.

ELAINE
Oh, no, I insist. Make yourself comfortable.

Elaine exits the room. Beth sits on the couch, looks around, and makes a few notes.

Elaine re-enters the room and sets down a tray holding a teapot and two cups. She sits and pours tea. Both women sip tea while they talk. Beth takes notes.

BETH
Thanks for speaking with me, Ms. McAuley. I'd like to take a look around your home today and ask you some questions about exposures you might have had.

ELAINE
Happy to help, sweetheart.

BETH
Do you have any pets?

ELAINE
Just my Frisky. He's at the doggy salon for his weekly grooming. I had a cat, but poor Poppy passed on, goodness, two years ago now.

BETH
Have you used any new products recently? Air fresheners, anything in the kitchen or bath?

ELAINE
Hmmm. Well, I did put in a new Glade Plug-In last week. Hawaiian Breeze. Doesn't it smell nice?

BETH
Does anyone in the home, or any visitors, smoke cigarettes or marijuana?

ELAINE
Certainly not. Now, my next-door neighbors, well. Let's just say some people never really left the sixties. The smoke drifts over to my porch. Makes it impossible to sit and enjoy my evenings.

BETH
Mind if I take a look at the household cleaners you use?

They get up and walk into the kitchen. Elaine indicates the cupboard beneath the sink. Beth opens the cupboard and takes notes.

BETH
Are you aware of any weed killers being used in the neighborhood?

ELAINE
The association books those people. But I've lived here five years and never had any issues after they did their spraying.

They walk into the dining room. The table is covered in scrapbooking paraphernalia: scissors, glue, cartons of patterned paper, rolls of decorative trim, a shiny green box, ticket stubs, photographs.

ELAINE
(smiling)
My hobby. To remember my wild and crazy trips with the girls!

Beth does a double take at a photo, glued to a sparkly scrapbook page, showing Elaine and two other elderly ladies wearing sunglasses and bikinis and holding tropical drinks.

BETH
Ahem. Well, I appreciate your time, ma'am. Would you be willing to complete a diary of public places you visited recently? It's online. I can send you the URL.

ELAINE
Sweetheart, what's a "URL"?

INT. PADEREWSKIS' HOUSE/LIVING ROOM - DAY

GEOFFREY and LORNA PADEREWSKI, a couple in their mid 70s, walk through their living room with Beth. A large, shaggy DOG follows them.

Nearly every surface in the room is covered with posterboard, markers, flyers, and petitions. Homemade protest signs, taped to yardsticks, lean against walls. On the floor are reams of paper, stacks of clipboards, a shiny green box, and containers full of stickers and buttons.

BETH
I take it you're involved in... political activities?

LORNA
Yes. That Senator Dankworth will stop at nothing to take away rights from women and LGBT folks.

GEOFFREY
He's pushing for another purge of the voter rolls. It's our civic responsibility to get that fool out of office. He's making the rest of us Boomers look bad.

BETH
Do you folks do any smoking, vaping, marijuana?

Geoffrey and Lorna look at each other.

LORNA
(to Geoffrey)
It's legal now, hon. Just tell her.

GEOFFREY
I enjoy a smoke from time to time. But it never caused me to cough up blood before. And when I got sick, I hadn't smoked in about a week.

BETH
Hey, no judgment here.

Beth makes a note.

LORNA
(to Beth)
Do you think toxic chemicals could be to blame? I saw some people on TV who got pneumonia after they used one of those Glade Plug-Ins.

BETH
Possibly. Did you use any new products in the home around the time you got sick? Cleaning supplies, potpourri, lotions?

GEOFFREY
We did have the house painted a couple of months ago.

LORNA
Wait, we did buy a new product. The hemorrhoid cream. Remember?

GEOFFREY
And that jock itch spray. That stuff really did the trick!

BETH
Well, you folks have been a big help! I'll send you the follow-up questionnaire tomorrow.

INT. KESSLERS' HOUSE/LIVING ROOM - DAY

JOHN and SHEILA KESSLER, a couple in their mid 70s, walk through their living room with Beth.

JOHN
(to Beth)
Yeah, I smoke. Same brand my whole life. She makes me go outside.

SHEILA
It's a nasty habit. I've never cared for it.

JOHN
I didn't get sick, though. Only Sheila did. Guess the cigarettes toughened up my lungs.

SHEILA
John, if you're the Marlboro Man, it's only because you've given them enough of your money to be a major stockholder.

They pause at an art easel, set up in a sunny corner.

BETH
Who's the painter?

SHEILA
That would be me.

JOHN
She's very good. Sold two landscapes just last month.

BETH
Where do you typically get your paint and supplies, ma'am?

SHEILA
Andy's Art, down on 10th.

They descend a set of stairs to a finished basement.

INT. KESSLERS' HOUSE/BASEMENT - DAY

Children's toys litter the room. A craft table sits against one wall. On its surface are markers, crayons, glue sticks, cartons of construction paper, a shiny green box, and half-completed drawings covered in glitter and cut-out shapes.

BETH
How old are your grandkids?

SHEILA
Let's see. Maisie is seven, the twins just turned six, and then our daughter has a two-year-old.

BETH
That's nice. Congratulations.

JOHN
Do you folks check for that Chinese drywall? Want to make sure we don't have any in the house.

BETH
We don't, sir, but if the home was built before 2000, don't worry.

JOHN
Good. What about that black mold?

SHEILA
There's no mold in this house, John. Remember, we had it checked because of Maisie's allergies.

BETH
Thank you, folks. Here's a copy of the follow-up questionnaire.

INT. COUNTY HEALTH DEPARTMENT OFFICE - DAY

Beth sits at a conference room table, laptop open, papers spread around. She appears deep in thought. Rick walks in and sits across from Beth.

BETH
It doesn't make sense.

RICK
Show me what you've got.

BETH
They have nothing in common. Messy house, clean house. Pets, no pets. Pot, no pot.

RICK
Asbestos?

BETH
No, the homes were all built after it was banned. Something in the environment? A pine tree disease?

RICK
How did the trees look?

BETH
I don't know. Green?

RICK
Insightful observation, Benson.

BETH
There must be a common element.

Rick passes a piece of paper to Beth.

RICK
I came to give you this. Details about those two kids who got sick.

BETH
(reading)
Kessler? Same last name as the folks I just interviewed. I think I'll go back over there and have another chat.

EXT. LONG PINES RETIREMENT COMMUNITY - DAY

Beth parks the health department vehicle in front of the Kesslers' house.

As she exits the car and steps onto the sidewalk, she sees a POSTMAN (40s) pushing a mail cart in her direction. Among the parcels in his cart is a shiny green box. She squints at the box as if it has jogged a memory.

> POSTMAN
> Afternoon! County Health Department, eh?

> BETH
> I'm investigating an illness that has cropped up in this area.

> POSTMAN
> Nothing I can catch from breathing the air, I hope!

Beth gestures at the green box.

> BETH
> That's certainly eye-catching. What company makes those?

> POSTMAN
> That's the Glitter Gurus. Popular product. I deliver their items quite a lot.

FLASHBACK MONTAGE - BETH REMEMBERS

-- ELAINE'S HOUSE – Beth spots a green box, and a glittery scrapbook page, on the dining room table.

-- THE PADEREWSKIS' HOUSE – Beth sees a green box on the floor in Geoffrey and Lorna's living room.

-- THE KESSLERS' HOUSE – Beth sees a green box on the craft table in the basement, next to a glittered piece of paper.

END FLASHBACK MONTAGE.

BACK TO SCENE

Beth's face now wears a look of recognition. She grabs the Postman's right hand in both of hers and shakes it.

> BETH
> Thank you!

Beth hurries to her car and speeds away.

Watching the car, the postman shakes his head, puzzled.

INT. PADEREWSKIS' HOUSE/LIVING ROOM - DAY

Geoffrey and Lorna sit on their couch watching TV. She flips through cookbooks. He taps at a laptop.

GOVERNOR HEATHER HAYNES (50s) appears on the TV screen. Geoffrey and Lorna glance up as she starts speaking.

> GOVERNOR HAYNES
> More than 20,000 types of glitter are sold commercially. Some newer varieties have particles small enough to cause lung infections when inhaled. That's why I've signed an executive order to outlaw so-called "glitter bombs" used by activists.

> GEOFFREY
> Well, damn. What're we going to do at Dankworth's rally next week?

Lorna holds up a cookbook, open to a page showing a cream pie recipe.

> LORNA
> How about an old-fashioned pie in the face?

INT. COUNTY HEALTH DEPARTMENT OFFICE - DAY

Beth exits the elevator and walks toward her cubicle.

Several of Beth's co-workers, including Rick, burst out from an office, greeting Beth and cheering. They slap her on the back and shake her hand.

> MALE CO-WORKER
> Nice detective work, Fisher!

                    DOLORES
            She was my hire. Just saying.

                FEMALE CO-WORKER
        Come on. Your cake's in the conference room!

The group moves down the hall. Rick walks beside Beth.

                      RICK
            Well done, Lieutenant Benson.

                      BETH
                     Thanks.

                      RICK
              So, is the perp in jail?

                      BETH
    Couldn't hold him. It was like he floated off into thin air.

Beth enters her cubicle and starts to set down her coat and purse. She stops short as she notices a stuffed unicorn sitting on her computer keyboard.

                      BETH
                      Rick!

Beth hurls a packet of tissues at Rick, who laughs and jumps to the side. She exits the cubicle after him.

The unicorn sits facing Beth as she walks away. It wears a T-shirt that reads "Law & Order: Glitter Victims Unit."

FADE OUT.

Mystery Outpost VII
by Vincent A. Alascia

Did you ever feel as though your mind had started to erode? Five days in and 400 million kilometers from earth, I'm slipping further and further into madness. I flipped through my notes, starting from the beginning. I received my current assignment from high up in the command chain. The only thing I knew was that my background in linguistics would come in handy. By the time I had arrived I had poured over all the details given me and still had no idea what I was doing here.

I stood in the airlock at the entry to Outpost VII. Years of space travel has made me something of a recycled air connoisseur. Moon Base Beta is the gold standard, you'd swear you were back on earth. There's some good air on Mars Station, but these small asteroid mining outposts are some of the worst. Every breath I drew came with the sting of stringent chemicals and not enough oxygen. The LEDs in the door frame turned from red to green and the grey titanium panel slid open as if it was a quarter of its weight.

"Welcome Inspector, to Strand Corps Selenium Mining Outpost Eight. I am Rebecca Walsh chief of operations."

"Nice to meet you Ms. Walsh."

"Please, call me Rebecca, Ms. Walsh was my mother."

"Very well. I'm inspector William Channing, you may call me Will."

She smiled. Her green eyes appeared more vibrant in the lighting as did her auburn hair. It was in a right bun at the top of her skull. The sides were shaved and when she spoke again, I noticed the stainless-steel dumbbell through her tongue. "I can show you to your quarters so that you can unwind."

"If it is okay with you, I'd like to see the artifact. I've had

37 hours of spaceflight to unwind."

"I understand. We don't get visitors out this far very often, but we've arranged comfortable quarters, I'll have your belongings sent there." She touched her wrist comm and instructed me to leave my bags at the airlock. "We have the artifact in one of our materials labs. It's right this way. You can leave your bags here and I'll have someone take them to your quarters."

I only had one case and my travel computer but felt it rude to say anything, so I left the case. I followed her from the airlock to the hallway on the left. "Your report says the artifact was found forty-seven meters below the surface."

"Yes, one of our survey drones came across it in a chasm we recently uncovered. Deep penetration scans must've missed it. To be honest if it weren't for an eagle-eyed operator, we'd never have seen it. Here we are, the lab is right here." She pressed several keys and the door opened with a whirring sound.

The light in the lab was much brighter than in the hall and my eyes blinked into an uneasy focus. The artifact sat on a metal table in the center of the empty room. "No one's been in here."

"Not since the bodies were found."

"Good." I approached the table. The artifact was an eight-sided polyhedron shape, a little larger than a human head. "Metallurgical analysis has not turned up anything?"

"It's no metal known to humankind."

As I looked over the surface of the thing, I could make you several characters etched on the surface. "These markings weren't in your report."

"I know. Corporate lawyers suggested we not reveal that much about the artifact yet. The mining charter gives us first rights to anything we find something like this and the bean counters on earth only see potential profit. Do you recognize the letters? It's weird, the same four symbols just repeat over and over."

I nodded. "It's a little beyond strange. Though I do not recognize them. And you ran them through your computer database."

Rebecca put her hands on her hips. "We're a mining outpost. That database only has minerals and compounds."

She was right. There was nothing I could use. I had to take scans and transmit them to the language database of the Tillerman Institute back on Earth. Unfortunately, with Jupiter between us it took several days for the transmission to arrive there. That gave me time to look at the deaths of the two materials scientists, Reginald Task and Vivian Connors. Right away I suspected an interpersonal matter. Miners spent eighteen to 48 months out here so it's not uncommon for relationships to blossom and wither. The position of the bodies made a murder-suicide look plausible.

"That's what I thought too," Dr. Richards said. She walked over to her view screen. "Then we looked at the tissue scans. First the bodies died seconds apart."

"Plausible if one wound was more fatal than the other."

"Deaths were instant. Plus, internal scans reveal that the damage worsened the deeper we looked."

"The report listed a hypersonic hammer as the weapon."

"We found the hammer in close proximity to the bodies, but this damage wasn't caused by it." She paused. "It seemed logical with all the crew disruptions we had been experiencing lately."

"I've read through the reports. I know a fair share of incidents are common but are you saying that this was out of the ordinary?"

"That's one way to put it. Something is tearing through this crew. From fights to anxiety, it's as if a switch went off," the doctor said.

She was right. Back in my room I looked over the outpost

incident logs, and they clearly pointed to some type of malaise running through the crew. It all started when the artifact came on board.

Over the next few days, my notes piled up and the interviews continued but I wasn't any closer to undertanding what happened, other than it was definitively not a murder-suicide. The door chime broke into my thoughts. "Come in."

Rebecca entered with a data screen. "This just came through coms for you." She looked at my notes and scribbles all over the table and bed. "Is this helping you get anywhere."

"It's a mess but helps me bounce from thought to thought," I said as I took the screen. I read through it twice and put it down.

"Were they able to translate it?"

I nodded. "The symbols are letters from an old Earth language that belonged to the Israelite people. It's the letters, Y,H,W,H, yodh he, waw, he. In standard English it's Yahweh, also referred to as the Tetrgrammaton, the holy name of God."

"God? We have some up here who are Sciterrian and see the universe as a living entity imbued with god-like properties. Are you saying this thing is a manifestation of that?"

"In Earth's ancient past it was not uncommon for people to worship beings that existed solely in their collective minds. Often it was a response to phenomena they could not understand."

"So how does an ancient earth language wind up on an artifact dug out of an asteroid floating in space?"

I could feel one hell of a headache coming on. "Well, there's only one of two possibilities. These ancient people had a space program that launched this artifact to this asteroid. The other that an alien being, from which this language originates, may have visited earth in the Middle Eastern desert some fifteen centuries ago."

Rebecca rubbed her forehead. The headache must be catching. "I suppose the first possibility is not likely. Though the second would prove that humans may have had contact with an alien species."

"They may not have realized what they had contact with. Still, it doesn't help us identify what this is, or how it may have killed those two scientists."

"Is that your conclusion?" Rebecca didn't try to hide the incredulity in her voice.

"I talked to everyone, looked over all the reports and autopsy results. Something in that room killed them and it wasn't that flipping hammer." I had just finished when the alert siren went off. In the last couple of days, it had become a regular occurrence.

Rebecca went to the comm panel and pressed the red button. "Opps, what's going on?"

"Becc," the strained voice of her second in command came over the comm. "You better get down here. Our reactor's gone critical."

CLASSIFIED

Strand Metals Corporation

Outpost VII Final Transmission

Time: 19:45.15 06.27.2158

This is Inspector William Channing. I am placing Outpost VII under immediate and permanent quarantine. Reactor critical. Sabotage. Radiation leak. No salvage. It's sentient. The damn thing is planning…

The Disappearance
by Mickey Collins

"Where's mom?" asked Cole.

"She's gone."

"Where did she go?"

"I don't know, all she left was this note: *Don't come looking for me.*"

The note was made up of cut-out letters from her collectible newspapers. She would never have destroyed those just to leave a message, no matter the importance.

"Was it because of me?"

"No, of course not. It's no one's fault. Let's finish the puzzle."

As if that would give closure.

Cole and his dad sat at the dining room table where Cole and his mother had completed the edges of the puzzle just yesterday and began moving inward.

Cole diligently looked for a piece, one that he knew the shape and color of. He created piles of rejects, tossed aside ones that didn't work. As the rejected piles grew bigger and his options grew smaller he worked more frantically. Pieces were thrown around, landing on the floor, falling off the edges of the table. His dad at first tried to grab the pieces and place them back on the table, only for Cole's wild movements to send them back down. The cat came over to see what new gifts had landed into his domain for his enjoyment. After a piece landed on his head, he skittered away.

As it had started, it ended. Cole couldn't find the piece he wanted. He shoved the half-complete puzzle to the ground, where it broke off into chunks.

Cole ran to his room. His dad followed behind. Cole slammed his door.

Why? why? Why? why? Why? why? Cole thought to himself. He threw his body into bed.

As his dad knocked, Cole yelled at him to go away.

Why mom? Cole wondered. Why not dad? All of the cool and interesting people in history that Cole cared about had lost their dads at a young age. It's what fueled their creativity. Why couldn't his dad have left instead?

He stared at the ceiling. There was a stain there that he didn't remember being there before. The longer he stared, the more he noticed it take on a shape. It looked like a laughing face. He blinked. It changed into a bear on its hind legs. A pear. A jack-o-lantern. Back to an amorphous blob.

Cole fell asleep cursing the fact that he would never be creative.

The Case of the Disposal
by Bob Selcrosse

I was awoken in the morning by the great boy detective, banging on the corrugated garage cover I called my front door. I put on my hat and rolled the door up to the ceiling.

'What time is it?' I said.

He handed me a vanilla ice cream. 'We've got to arrive early,' he said.

'Arrive where?' I said.

He stood over the circus poster on the table, eating his own vanilla ice cream. 'The crux of this case.'

'You found the woman?'

He gave no indication he'd heard me. 'The circus will come tomorrow,' he said. 'Whether we like it or not.'

'The circus can't take everything away,' I said. When he stood next to things, it was really clear he was a boy. And I remembered then that he was too young to have ever seen the circus.

I shut and locked my garage and we set out for our next link in the chain.

We arrived at a blue-gabled house with two-stories and stepped up the few concrete steps to the door. This time I rang the doorbell. Waiting, I realized I needed something to smooth out the lingering vanilla of the ice cream. I tapped the great boy detective's shoulder with the back of my fingers.

He checked his pockets, front, back, shirt. Finally from his jacket, he gave me a caramel. I untwisted the plastic and popped the caramel in my mouth. The great boy detective was always good for a caramel.

When the man opened the door, he looked at us both. He wore a sweater over his shirt. And his face was pink like he got easily frustrated.

'Who are you?' he said.

'We're your detectives,' said the great boy detective.

I smiled, the caramel glued to the back of my teeth.

The man looked up the street, then down the street, then dragged us inside and shut his door. 'I have a problem with the disposal unit,' he said. 'I can't explain it.'

He led us to the kitchen where every surface was stacked with dishes, pots and pans and puddles of food, which looked already digested and spit up, scattered the floor.

'Watch,' he said. He took a plate with some residual red sauce and scraped it into the sink with a knife, then he opened the faucet and flipped on a switch. He promptly turned both off again, but what had already drained in shot forcefully back up, a small geyser. *'Whore! Cocksucker!'* followed a voice.

I felt as if I were buried alive. The great boy detective, however, treated it calmly. 'May I take a look under the sink?' he said.

The color in the man's face drained and settled about his neck. He pushed his eyes with his thumb and finger. 'I'm ashamed,' he said. 'It's embarrassing for me.'

The great boy detective opened the cupboards and the man and I stooped down to watch. Behind bottles of cleaner, a plunger and gloves, there was the trunk of a man, arms torso, visible up to the edge of his neck. And the trunk of course was attached to legs. One leg extended awkwardly out, while the other remained tucked, so the upper half arranged crooked. I tried to get a better look, but still the mouth remained hidden. I saw only the Adam's apple, which was faintly bulged and purple.

'It's very clear,' said the great boy detective, emerging. 'Do you keep his antacids nearby?'

'Of course,' said the man. He opened a drawer and stepped away to leave the boy at it.

Rifling through, the great boy detective produced a near-full role of candy-flavored antacids, and popped a few in his mouth. After a moment, chewing, the great boy detective blew a sizable pink bubble.

The man looked utterly shocked.

'These aren't prescription I take it,' said the great boy detective, rifling through the drawer a second time.

'No,' said the man. 'But the pharmacist always recommends them. I would never. You have to trust me. I-'

But the great boy detective remained unconcerned. Finally, he retrieved a near empty roll of mint-candy antacids from the drawer and examined them closely. He pinched one, but the coating remained steadily intact.

'*Bitch! Whore! Cock!*' came the voice from under the sink.

The great boy detective removed the penultimate tablet and dropped it in the hole the sink. A few moments later, he flicked on the sink. He took up the same plate of red sauce and pushed a few knife-worths into the sink. When he turned off the water, there was at first a large gurgle, a few coughs, but no word, no profanity.

'Throw all the rest out,' said the great boy detective, indicating the drawer full of antacid foils. 'You have only this left.' He handed him the final tablet, the foil scrap jutting out like a tail. 'My associate and I will go and speak to the pharmacist.'

The man took the great boy detective's hands in his own and bowed his head low. 'I'm so ashamed,' he said. 'So ashamed.'

We saw ourselves out.

This time we went to the boardwalk. The ocean was black except for red dappling light in the waves. The boardwalk had boats, but it also had a carnival. People didn't like to come to it, and it was usually dead. Tonight however there were six people riding the spinning swing set. Its red and white light tickled the ocean.

We walked with cotton candy. Mine was pink and the great boy detective's was blue. He gobbled his heartily. But I could only pick at mine.

'She could be dead by now,' I said.

'Who's that?' His lips, tongue and teeth were all stained blue.

'The missing woman.'

He held a hand over one eye and said, '*Arrrr*,' The sugar had hit him.

'This is serious,' I said. 'Someone's sister is in line for being killed and the circus begins in less than twenty-four hours, we're not one step closer than we were yesterday-'

He spun around and pointed at my feet. 'Not one step closer,' he said. 'If you do, you'll end the whole mystery.'

So much had been taken away from him. He stood as if he were about to play hopscotch.

But then I saw it. In the distance behind him. The same balloons. The same as before. The balloon salesman was riding the Ferris wheel, going up and up and up.

We ran.

'I want one,' said the great boy detective, catching his breath. 'I want a balloon.'

The balloon salesman was nearing the apex of the Ferris wheel. I had enough money for every balloon.

'Just you wait,' I said. 'We'll-'

But as the balloons rounded over the top, the balloon man and his balloons lifted into the sky. The balloons brightened in moonlight and the man drifted over the sea. We watched him become smaller in the distance, until, like the day star finally blinks out, he vanished.

The great boy detective's watch began beeping. 'Don't worry about it,' he said. 'I'll see you tomorrow.'

I stood alone on the boardwalk and listened to the waves and calliope music. This time, there was no crumpled up poster rolling around in the dark. But I did not dare look in the sky. I felt as if a constellation were boring its eyes into me.

Bios

Vincent A. Alascia
Vincent A. Alascia is the author of, "The Hole In Your Mind," "Undead Heart," "In the Presence of Gods," and, "Xristos: Chosen of God," available on Kindle and paperback as well as works that have appeared in anthologies and online. Originally an East Coast native, he makes his home in the Portland Oregon area with his wife. Vincent has been a librarian for over 15 years and is also a musician. He is currently working on a Steampunk Horror novel and a guide to reading Tarot. Website: www.vaalascia.com

Roger Camp
Roger Camp is the author of three photography books including the award winning *Butterflies in Flight*, Thames & Hudson, 2002 and *Heat*, Charta, Milano, 2008. His work has appeared on the covers of numerous journals including *The New England Review, Southwest Review, Vassar Review* and *Lumina*. His work is represented by the Robin Rice Gallery, NYC. More of his work may be seen on Luminous-Lint.com.

Mark D Cart
Seventeen years I've been a bookseller. Once I was laureate of Portsmouth and twice a finalist for New Hampshire.

Yuan Changming
Yuan Changming hails with Allen Yuan from poetrypacific.blogspot.ca. Credits include eleven Pushcart nominations, nine chapbooks as well as publications in *Best of the Best Canadian Poetry* (2008-17), & BestNewPoemsOnline, among others.

Nicole Chvatal
Nicole Chvatal writes property deeds and lives in Maine. Her work has appeared in *The Maine Sunday Telegraph, LEON, Pilgrimage* and *Verseweavers*. She is a graduate of the MFA Program for Writers at Warren Wilson College.

Mickey Collins
~~Mickey rights wrongs. Mickey wrongs rites.~~ Mickey writes words, sometimes wrong words but he tries to get it write.

Mike Corrao
MIKE CORRAO is the author of three novels, *MAN, OH MAN* (Orson's Publishing); *GUT TEXT* (11:11 Press) and *RITUALS PERFORMED IN THE ABSENCE OF GANYMEDE* (11:11 Press); one book of poetry, *TWO NOVELS* (Orson's Publishing); two plays, *SMUT-MAKER* (Inside the Castle) and *ANDROMEDUSA* (Forthcoming - Plays Inverse); and three chapbooks, *AVIAN FUNERAL MARCH* (Self-Fuck); *MATERIAL CATALOGUE* (Alienist) and *SPELUNKER* (Schism - Neuronics). Along with earning multiple Best of the Net nominations, Mike's work has been featured in publications such as *3:AM*, *Collagist*, *Always Crashing*, and *Denver Quarterly*. He lives in Minneapolis.

Ben Crowley
Ben Crowley is from Pittsburgh, Pennsylvania. He is happy to get back to writing because he has already paid a kidney, a finger and a thumb to Deep Overstock and is considering dishing out three molars. Ben used to sort books for the Amazon warehouse, in our beautiful backcountry of western Pittsburgh. Now he drives a truck, but he's still selling books at whatever diner, truckstop or seedy hotel he finds himself in.

Holly Day
Holly Day (hollylday.blogspot.com) has been a writing instructor at the Loft Literary Center in Minneapolis since 2000. Her poetry has recently appeared in *Hubbub*, *Grain*, and *Third Wednesday*, and her newest books are *The Tooth is the Largest Organ in the Human Body* (Anaphora Literary Press), *Book of Beasts* (Weasel Press), *Bound in Ice* (Shanti Arts), and *Music Composition for Dummies* (Wiley).

Lynette G. Esposito
Lynette G. Esposito has been published in *Poetry Quarterly*, *Inwood Indiana*, *Walt Whitman Project*, *That Literary Review*, *North of Oxford*, and others. She was married to Attilio Esposito.

Robert Eversmann
Robert Eversmann works for Deep Overstock.

Kate Falvey
My work has been fairly widely published in journals and anthologies; in a very deeply understocked collection of poems, *The Language of Little Girls* (David Robert Books); and in two chapbooks. I edit the *2 Bridges Review*,

published through City Tech/CUNY, where I teach, and am an associate editor for the *Bellevue Literary Review*.

In ancient times, in a city that was once Los Angeles, I worked in Partridge Bookstore stocking shelves and fending off what used to be mildly termed advances. I got paid mostly in books and experience, not all of the bookstore kind. Other book business: I amassed and lost over a thousand books in a hurricane eight years ago, but still have nearly that many left high and dry. Yet still I moan through my hallways, I have nothing to read....And still I lament the ones that got hurtled and washed away. Even the ones that deserved it.

L. Fid

L. Fid is a member of a pseudonymous arts collective dedicated to world domination. The adventures of Nutter, Pel, Stealer, Fran, J and the Situationists are entirely fictional, though L. Fid did once work at an airport bookstore with a part-time private investigator named Tony.

Joe Giordano

Joe Giordano was born in Brooklyn. He and his wife Jane now live in Texas. Joe's stories have appeared in more than one hundred magazines including *The Saturday Evening Post*, and *Shenandoah*. His novels, *Birds of Passage, An Italian Immigrant Coming of Age Story* (2015), and *Appointment with ISIL, an Anthony Provati Thriller* (2017) were published by Harvard Square Editions. Rogue Phoenix Press published *Drone Strike* (2019) and his short story collection, *Stories and Places I Remember* (2020).

Joe was among one hundred Italian American authors honored by Barnes & Noble to march in Manhattan's 2017 Columbus Day Parade. Read the first chapter of Joe's novels and sign up for his blog at http://joe-giordano.com/

Lindsay Granduke

Lindsay Granduke is a full-time bookseller, part-time folklore enthusiast, and one-time anime voice actor. She graduated from Rollins College in Winter Park, Florida where she received the Academy of American Poets Prize for her poem "Vaulting Up" and the van den Berg Award for her short story "Where's Your Goddess?". When she's not writing, you can find her in an independent bookstore, writing about Bluebeard, or spending way too much time on Twitter @lindsaygranduke.

Charles Halsted

I am a retired academic physician. My poetry education consists of my attendance at six different 3-day workshops in California, Oregon, and New Mexico as well as twelve consecutive 10-week online courses provided by established American poets. I spent my early childhood in Dedham,

MA, then moved to Los Angeles, CA where I attended high school. My subsequent education consisted of four years at Stanford University, medical school at the University of Rochester School of Medicine, internship and residency training at Cleveland Metropolitan General Hospital, and further specialty training at Johns Hopkins Hospital in Baltimore, MD. My obligatory military service was met by two years at the US Naval Medical Research Unit #3 in Cairo, Egypt. After fifty years as a medical doctor, I retired in 2015 and began to write poetry. Thus far, I have published three poetry books with two more in progress, and more than eighty poems in thirty-five different poetry journals.

NANCY HAYES
Nancy Hayes is the mother of a Powell's Bookstore bookseller.

KARLA LINN MERRIFIELD
Karla Linn Merrifield has 14 books to her credit, including the 2019 full-length book *Athabaskan Fractal: Poems of the Far North* from Cirque Press. She is currently working on a poetry collection, *My Body the Guitar*, to be published in December 2021 by Before Your Quiet Eyes Publications Holograph Series.

JEN MIERISCH
Jen Mierisch's first job was at a public library, where her boss frequently caught her reading the books she was supposed to be shelving. Her work has appeared or is forthcoming in HAVOK, Horla, Funny Pearls, Little Old Lady (LOL) Comedy, and elsewhere. She lives, works, and writes just outside Chicago, Illinois, USA. Read more at www.jenmierisch.com.

TIMOTHY ARLISS OBRIEN
Timothy Arliss OBrien is an interdisciplinary artist in music composition, writing, and visual arts. His goal is to connect people to accessible new music that showcases virtuosic abilities without losing touch of authentic emotions. He has premiered music with The Astoria Music Festival, Cascadia Composers, Sound of Late's 48 hour Composition Competition and ENAensemble's Serial Opera Project. He also wants to produce writing that connects the reader to themselves in a way that promotes wonder and self realization. He has published several novels (Dear God I'm a Faggot, They), several cartomancy decks for divination (The Gazing Ball Tarot, The Graffiti Oracle, and The Ink Sketch Lenormand), and has written for Look Up Records (Seattle), Our Bible App, and Deep Overstock: The Bookseller's Journal. He has also combined his passion for poetry with his love of publishing and curates the podcast The Poet Heroic and he also hosts the new music podcast Composers Breathing. He also showcases his psychedelic

makeup skills as the phenomenal drag queen Tabitha Acidz.
Check out more of his writing, and his full discography at his website: www.timothyarlissobrien.com

BOB SELCROSSE
Bob Selcrosse grew up with his mother, selling books, in the Pacific Northwest. He is now working on a book about a book. It is based in the Pacific Northwest. The book is *The Cabinet of Children*.

SHERRY SHAHAN
Sherry Shahan watches the world from behind; whether in the hub of Oxford, an alley in Havana, or alone in a squat hotel room in Paris; whether with a 35 mm camera or an iPhone. Her photos have appeared in *The Los Angeles Times*, *Christian Science Monitor*, *Fourth River*, *Moon Shadow Press*, and forthcoming from *Gargoyle*, *Montana Mouthful*, *Literary Mama* and *Ephimila*. She holds an MFA from Vermont College of Fine Arts.

JIHYE SHIN
Jihye Shin is a 1.5-generation Korean-American bookseller in Florida. Her work focuses on the poetics of the analog-digital, liminial and futurist differences. She is also the creator of a text-based interactive game called Goodnight, Starlight. Her professional website is www.jihyeshin.ink.

JONATHAN VAN BELLE
Jonathan van Belle is a Philosophy Content Creator for Outlier.org, an online education platform. He previously worked as a bookseller at Powell's City of Books. Jonathan is the author of several books, including *Zenithism*, published by Deep Overstock.

Z.B. WAGMAN
Z.B. Wagman is a writer based in Portland, Oregon. He has two dogs that take most of his attention. When not bribing the dogs out into the rain, he can be found at the Beaverton City Library, where he finds much inspiration for his writing.

ALEX WERNER
Alex is a lifelong reader and writer of mystery stories who was raised on Arthur Conan Doyle and Agatha Christie. She is a collector of books with inscriptions written to other people. She cherishes these books and their secrets. Contact @alexwerner20 on Twitter to contribute a book to the collection.

NICHOLAS YANDELL

Nicholas Yandell is a composer, who sometimes creates with words instead of sound. In those cases, he usually ends up with fiction and occasionally poetry. He also paints and draws, and often all these activities become combined, because they're really not all that different from each other, and it's all just art right?

When not working on creative projects, Nick works as a bookseller at Powell's Books in Portland, Oregon, where he enjoys being surrounded by a wealth of knowledge, as well as working and interacting with creatively stimulating people. He has a website where he displays his creations; it's nicholasyandell.com. Check it out!

All rights to the works contained in this journal belong to their respective authors. Any ideas or beliefs presented by these authors do not necessarily reflect the ideas or beliefs held by Deep Overstock's *editors.*

CPSIA information can be obtained
at www.ICGtesting.com
Printed in the USA
FSHW011429250321
79780FS